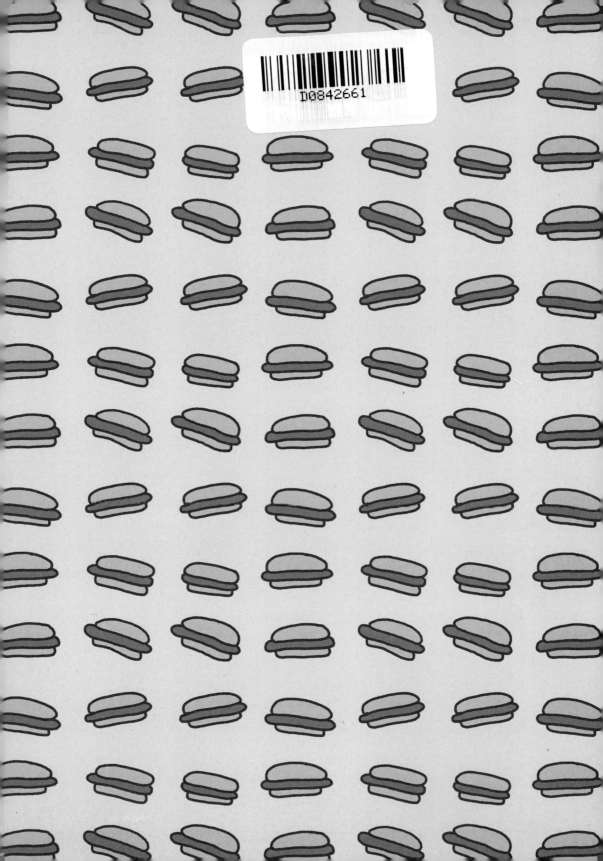

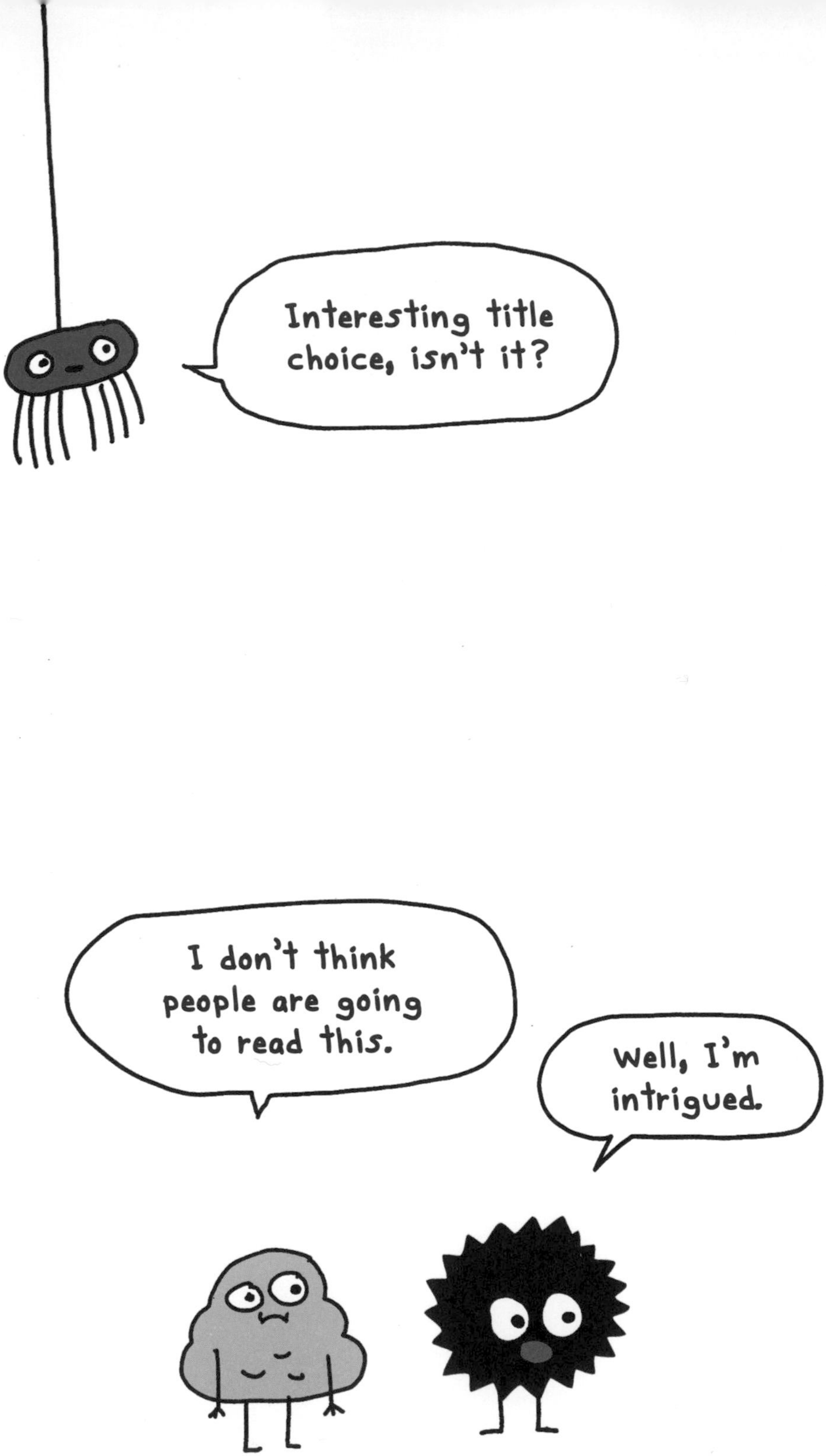
Interesting title choice, isn't it?
I don't think people are going to read this.
Well, I'm intrigued.

THE WORST BOOK EVER

ELISE GRAVEL • ENFANT

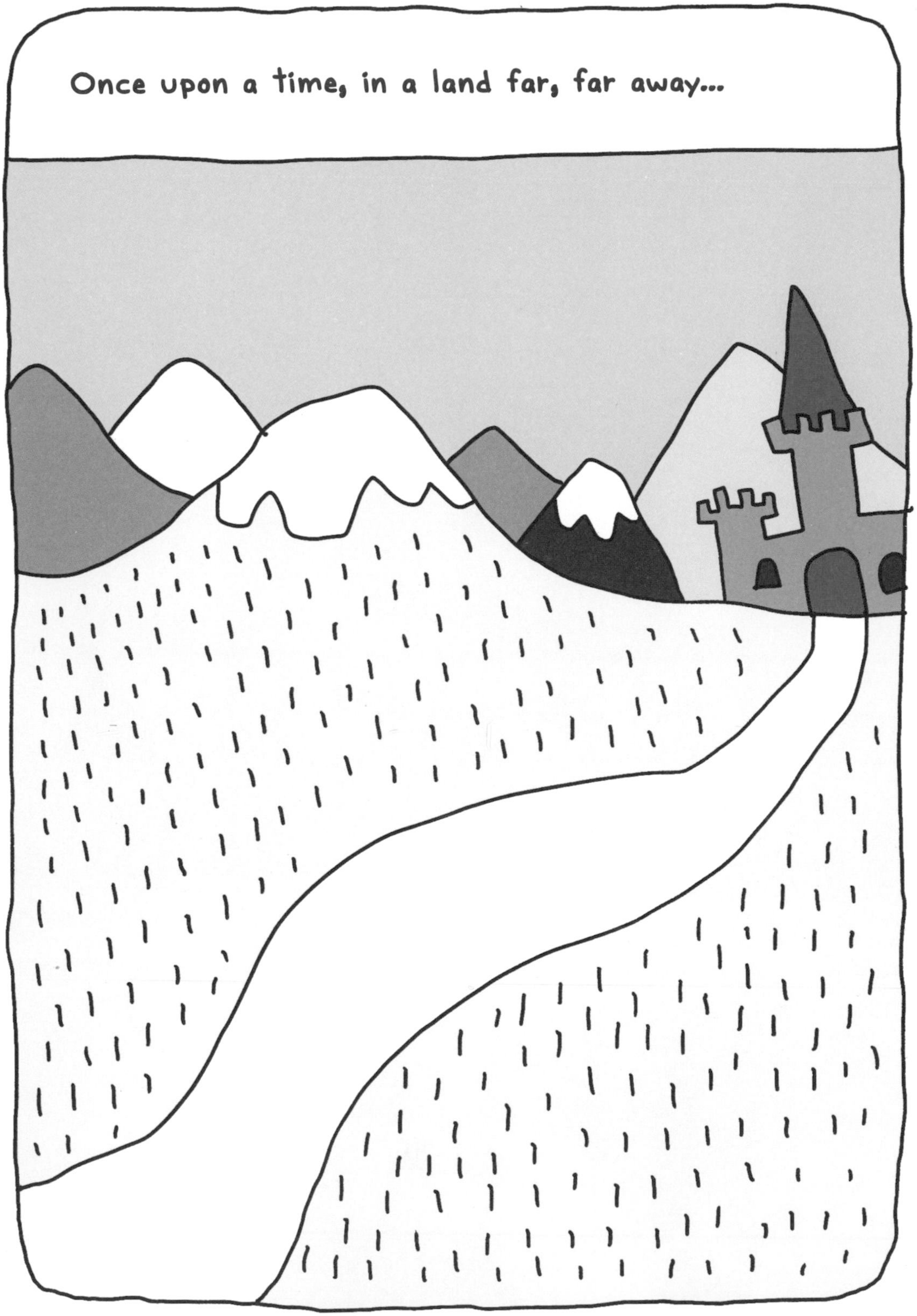
Once upon a time, in a land far, far away...

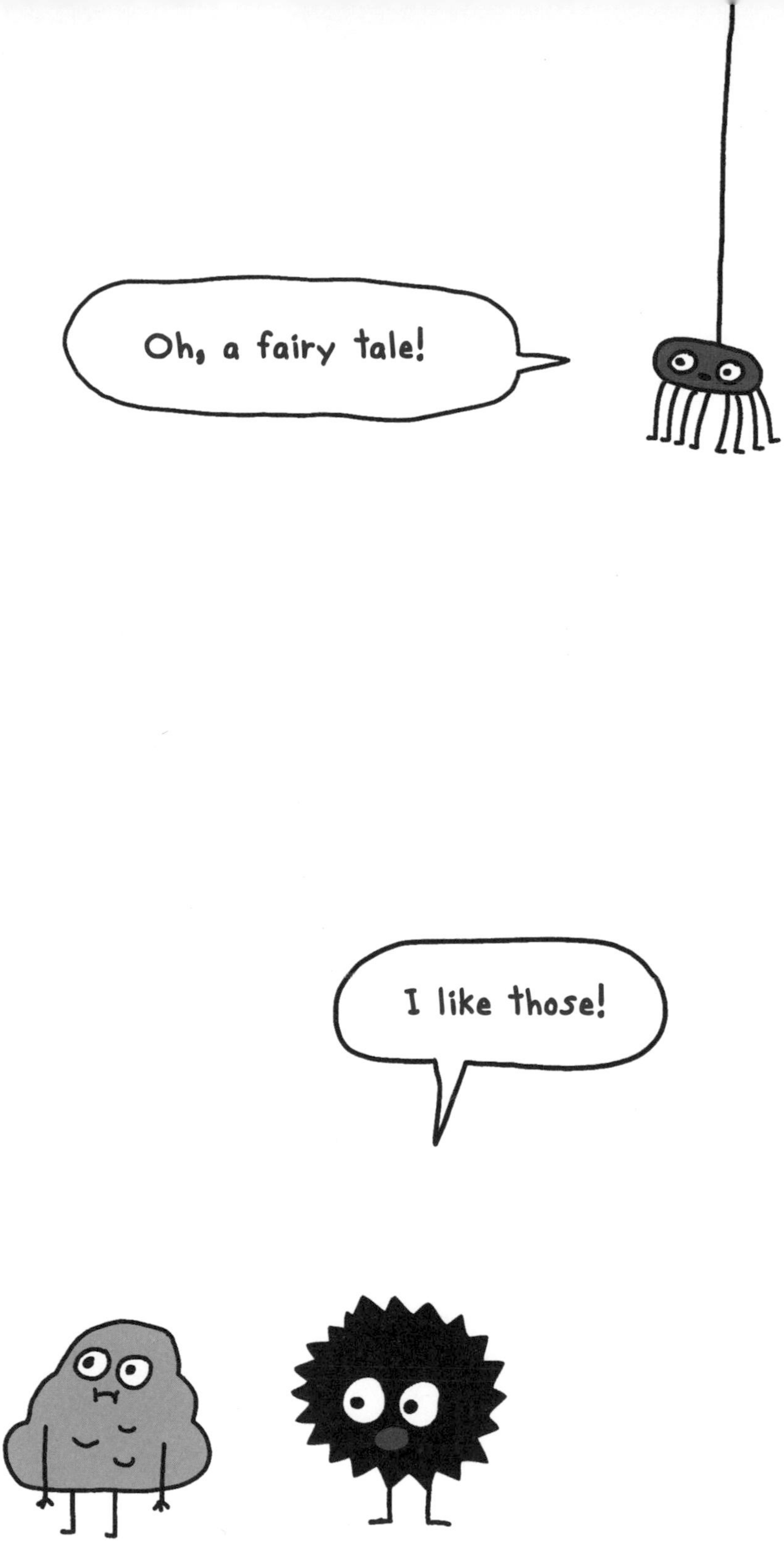
Oh, a fairy tale!
I like those!

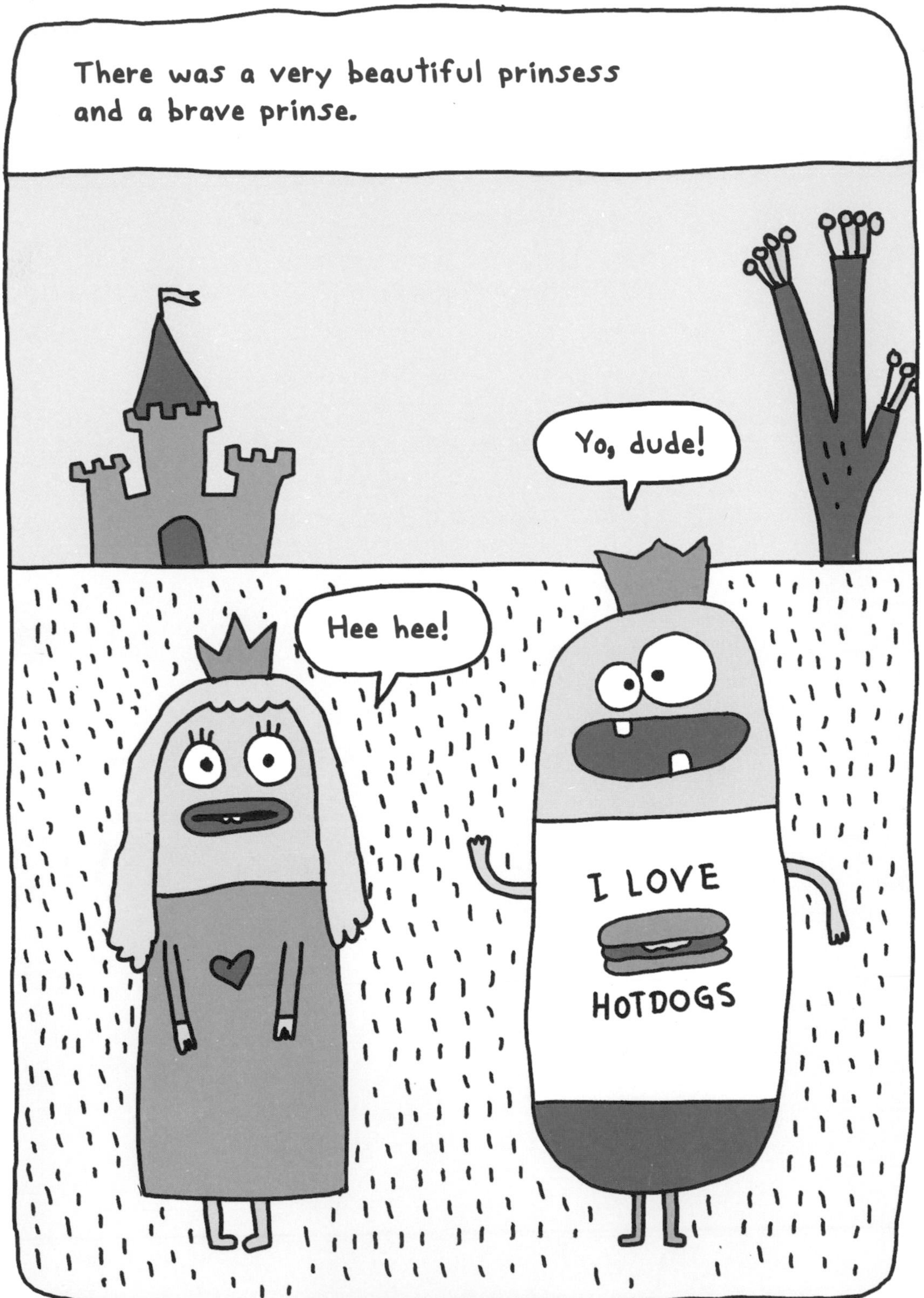
There was a very beautiful prinsess and a brave prinse.
Yo, dude!
Hee hee!
I LOVE HOTDOGS

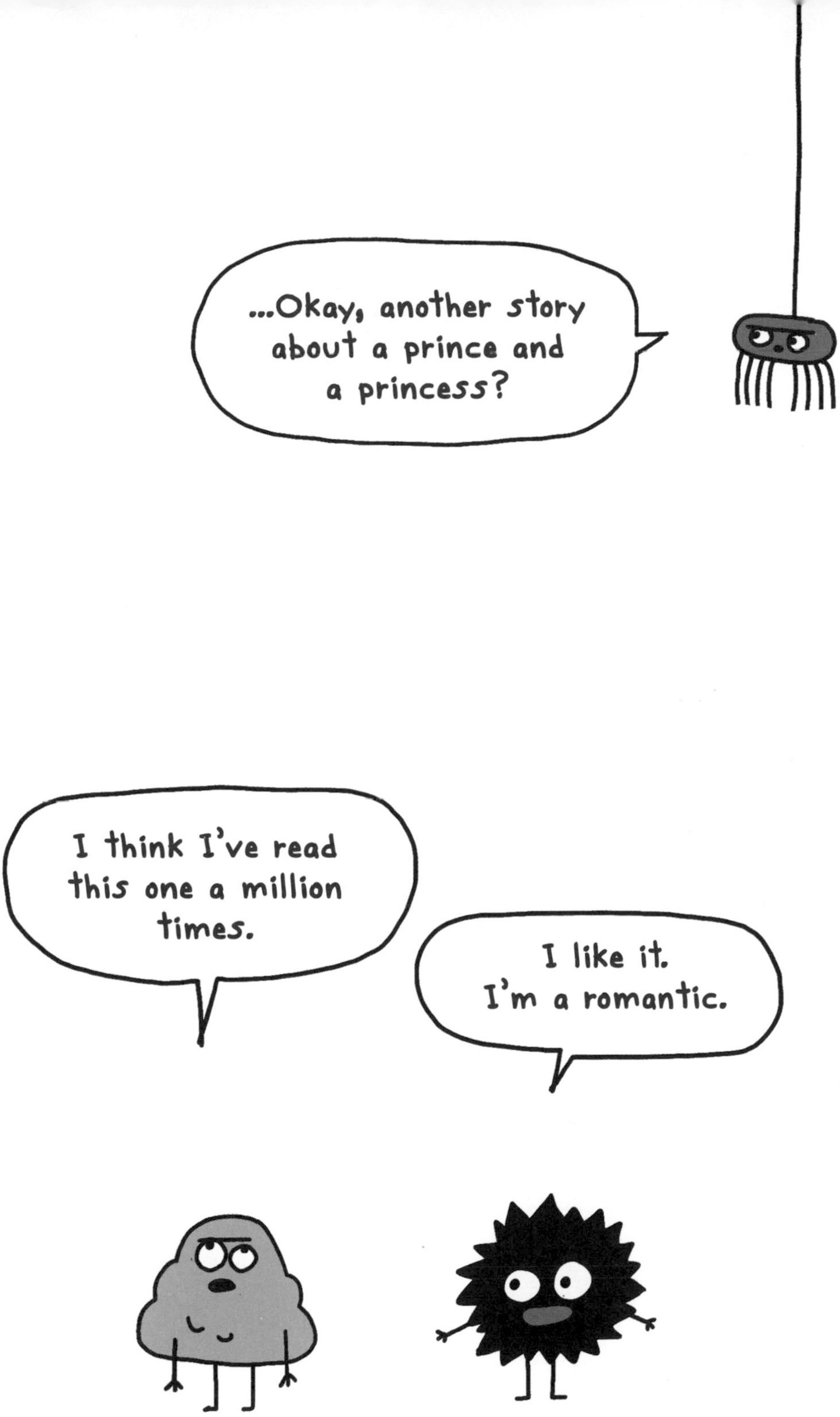
...Okay, another story about a prince and a princess?
I think I've read this one a million times.
I like it. I'm a romantic.

The prinsess lived in a magnificent castle.

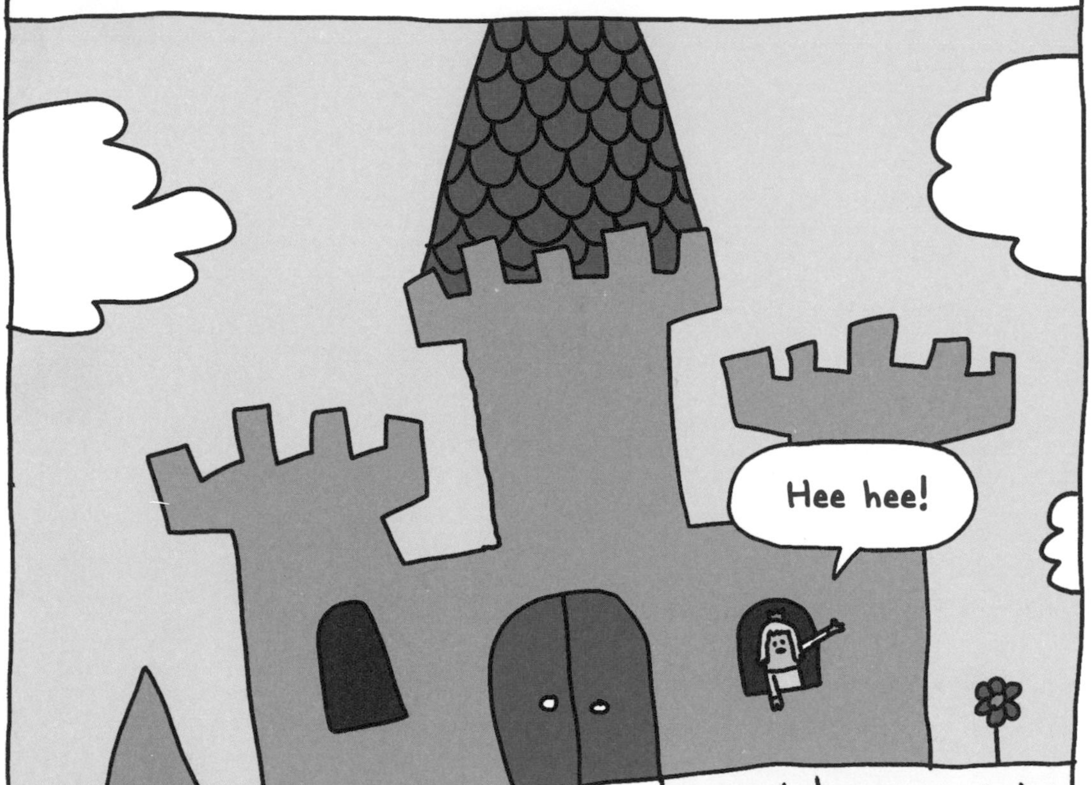

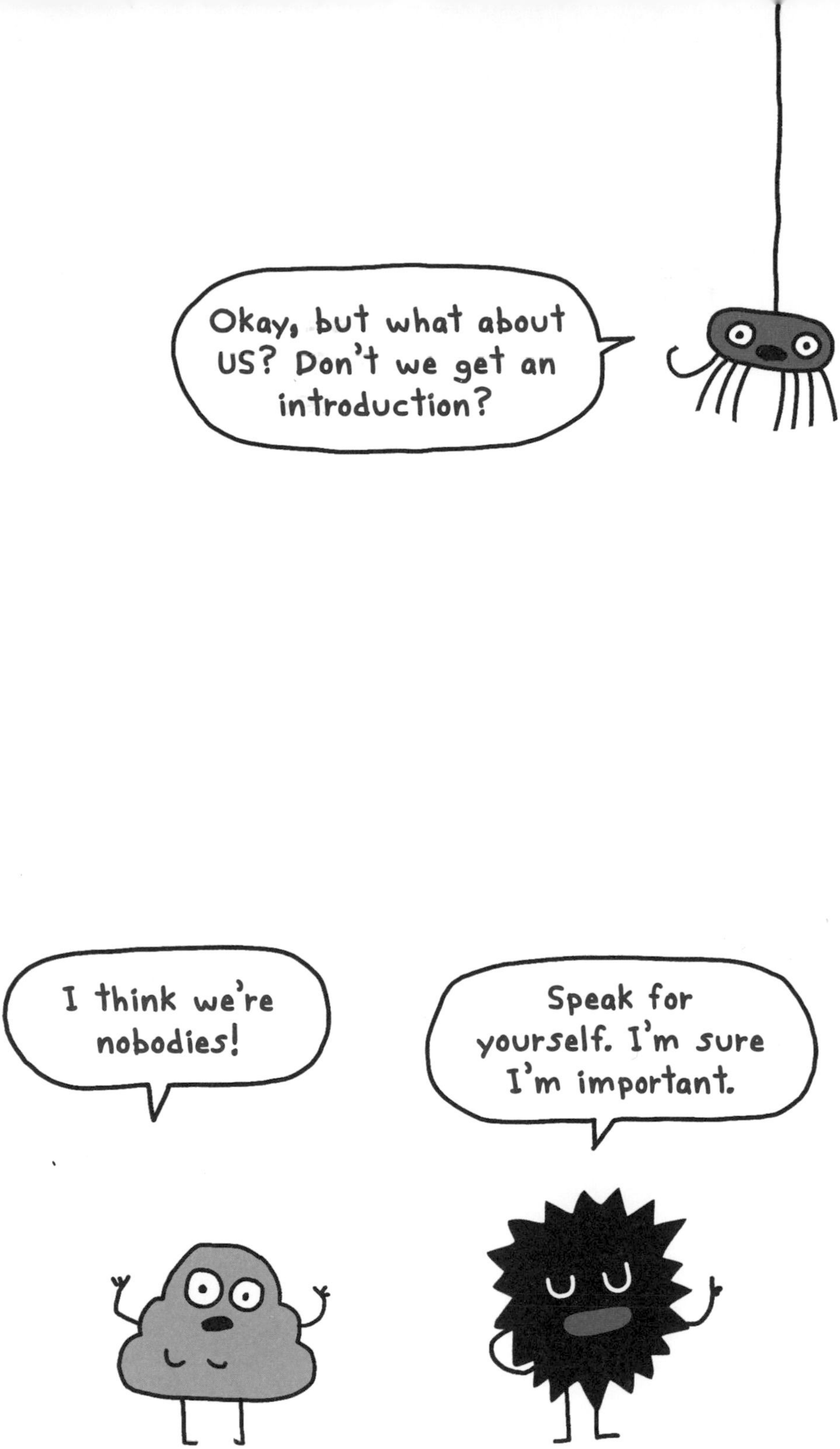
Okay, but what about US? Don't we get an introduction?
I think we're nobodies!
Speak for yourself. I'm sure I'm important.

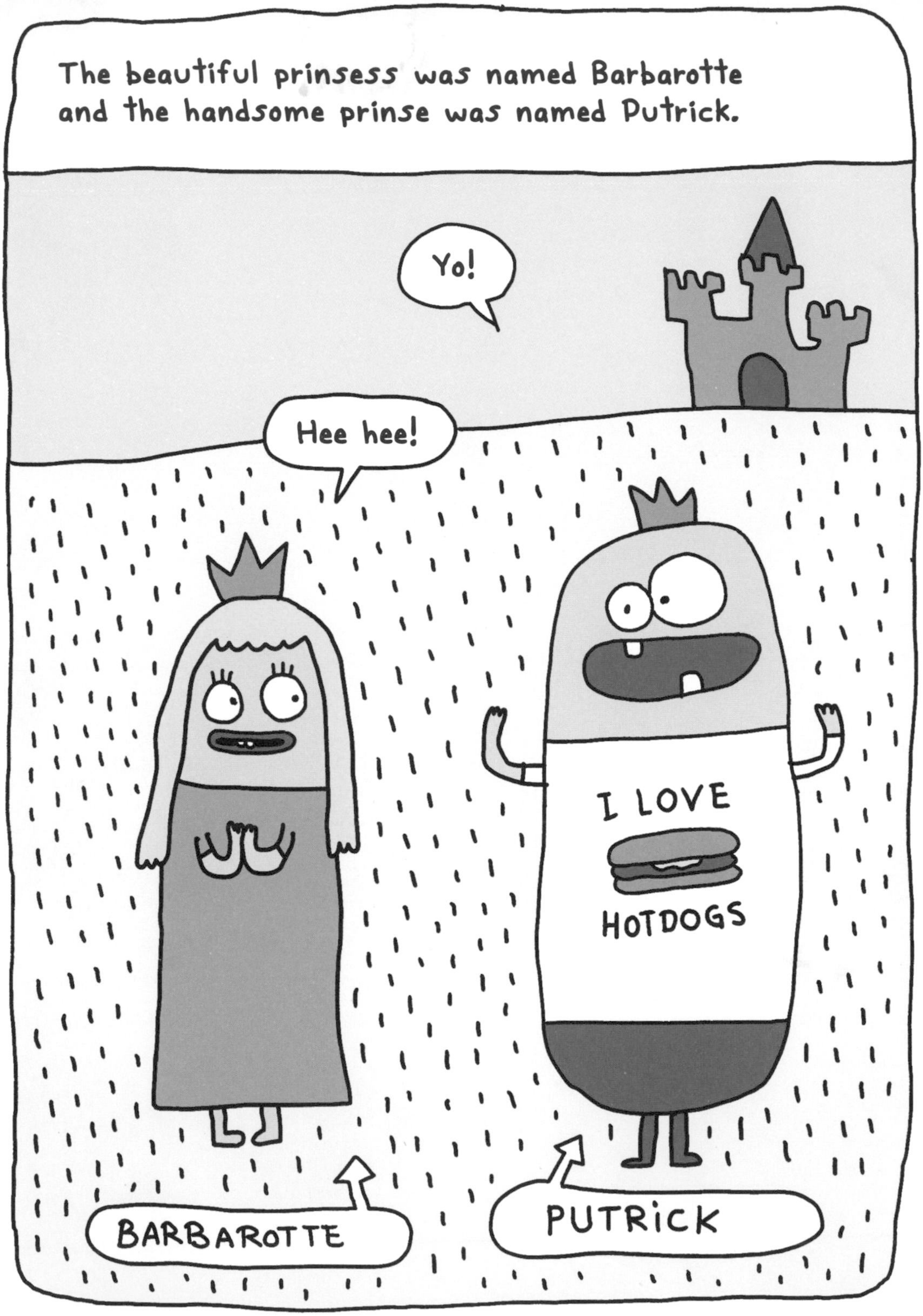
The beautiful prinsess was named Barbarotte and the handsome prinse was named Putrick.
Yo!
Hee hee!
I LOVE
HOTDOGS
BARBAROTTE
PUTRICK

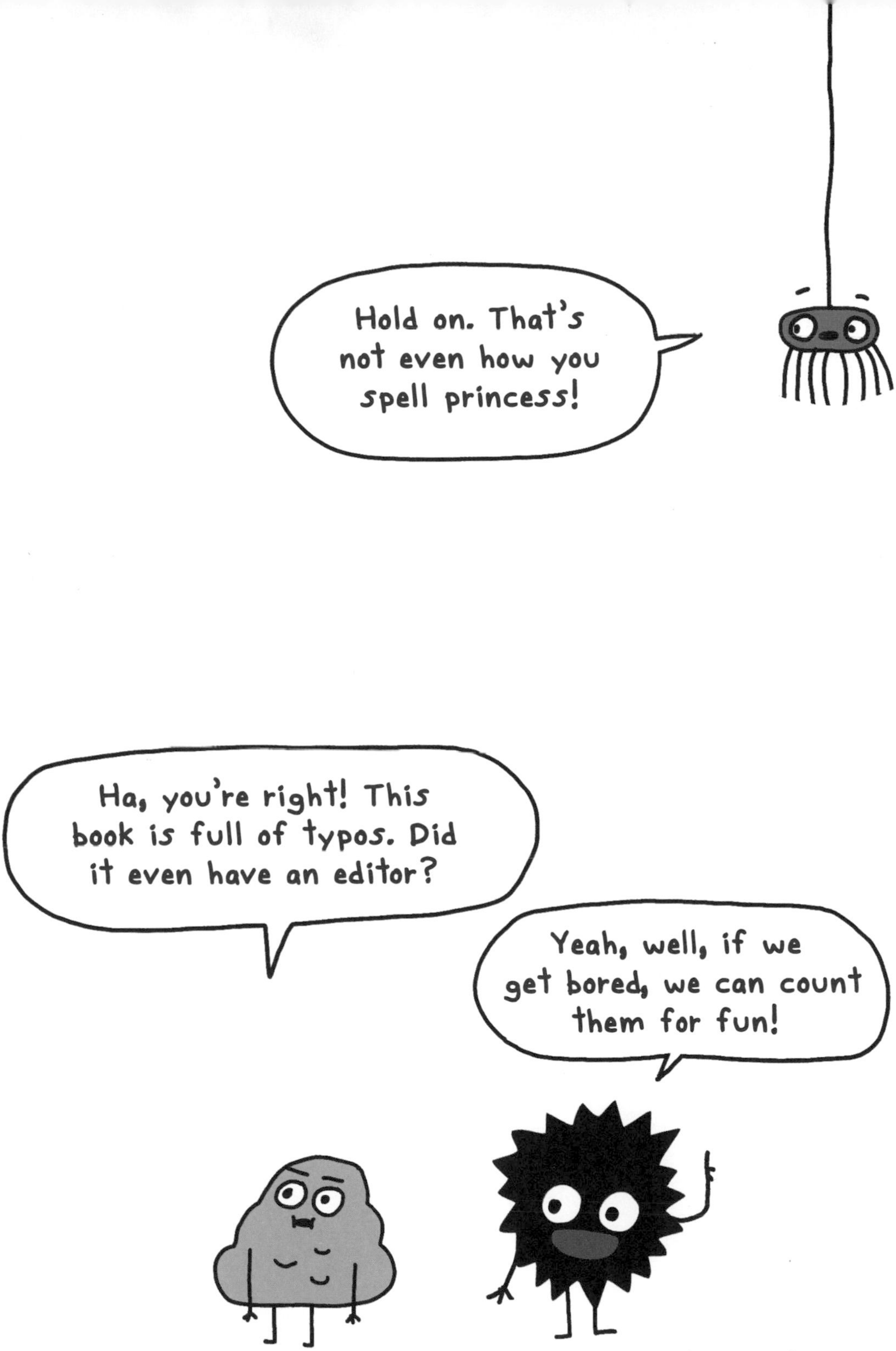
Hold on. That's not even how you spell princess!
Ha, you're right! This book is full of typos. Did it even have an editor?
Yeah, well, if we get bored, we can count them for fun!

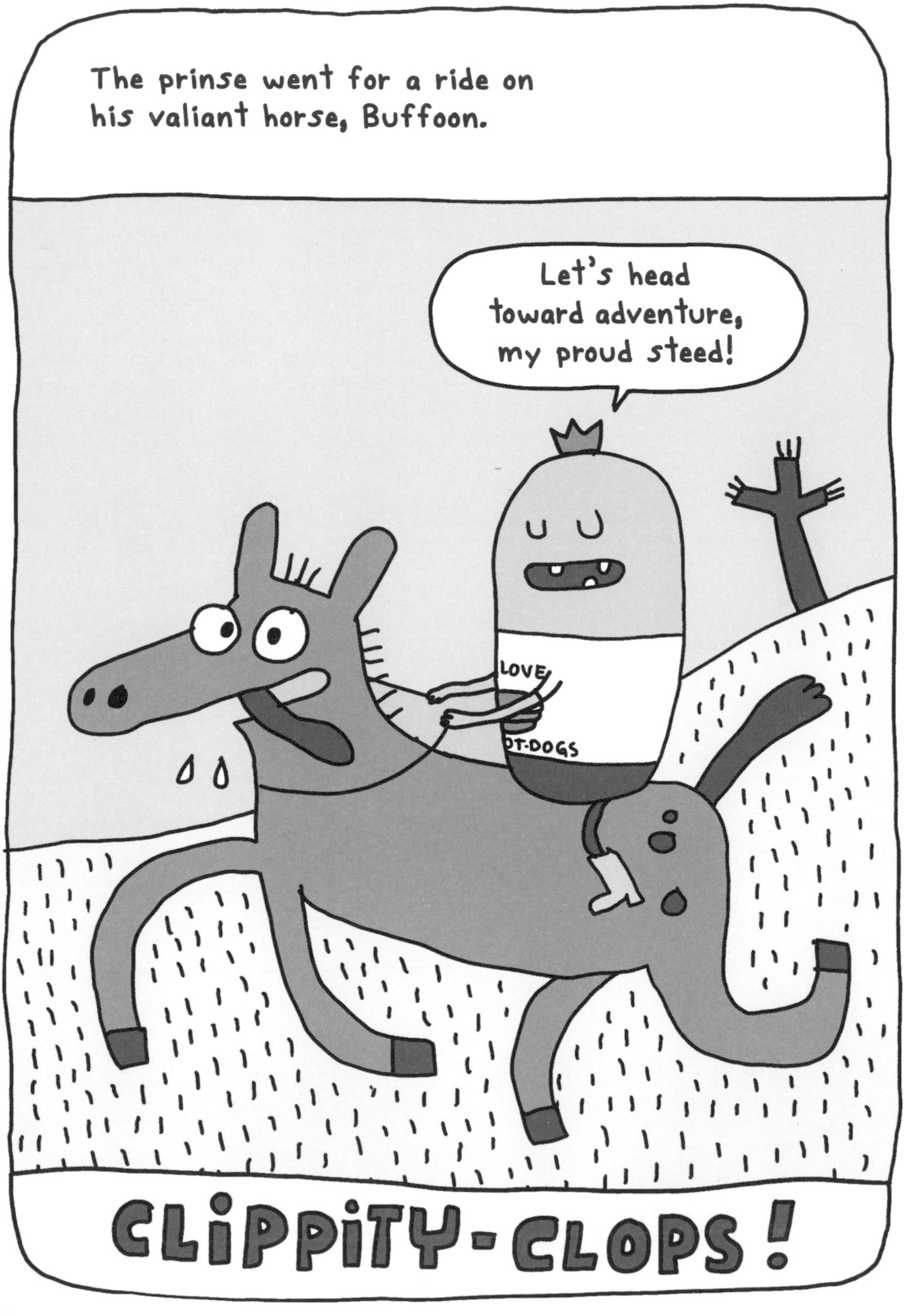
The prinse went for a ride on his valiant horse, Buffoon.
Let's head toward adventure, my proud steed!
LOVE
OT-DOGS
CLIPPITY-CLOPS!

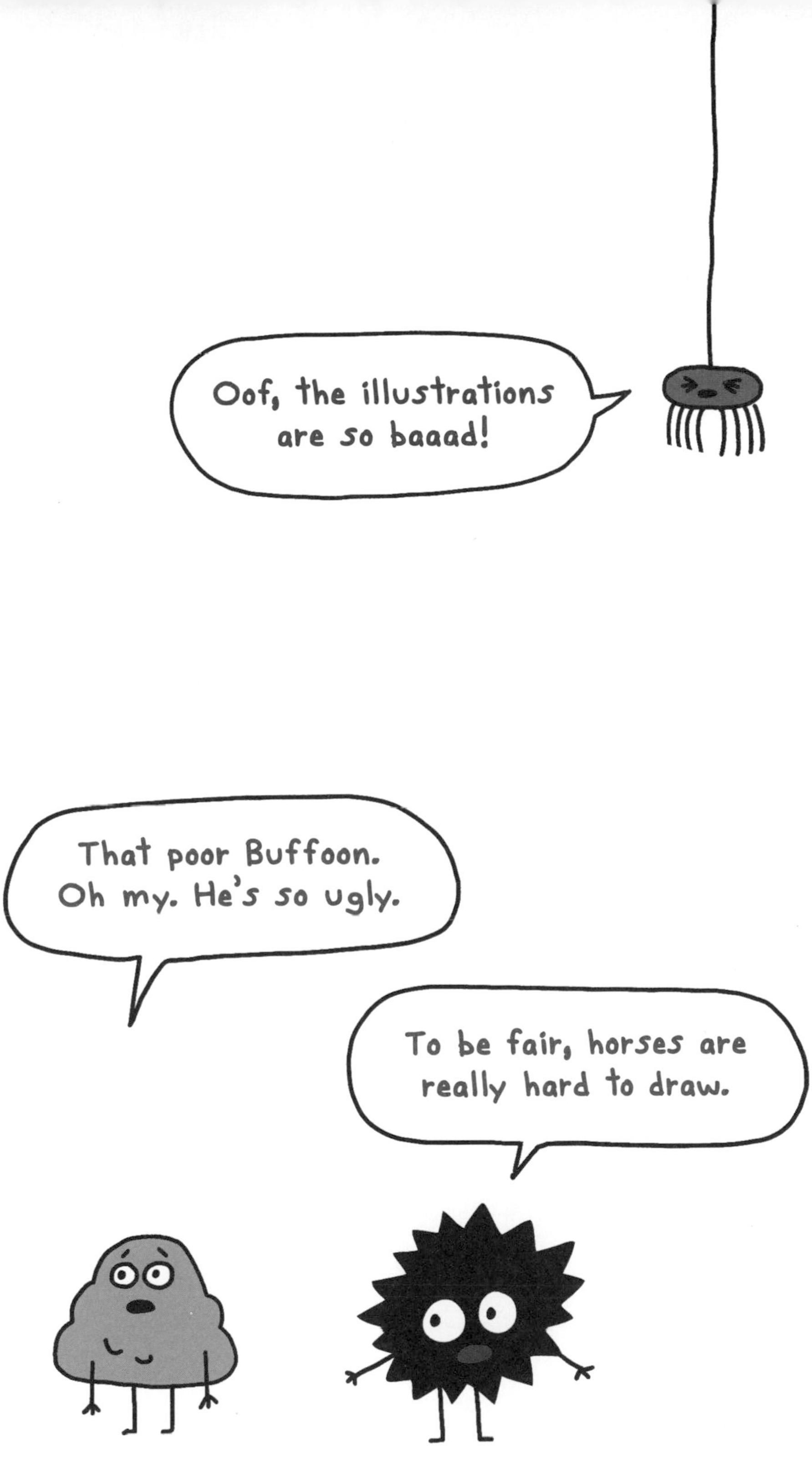
Oof, the illustrations are so baaad!
That poor Buffoon. Oh my. He's so ugly.
To be fair, horses are really hard to draw.

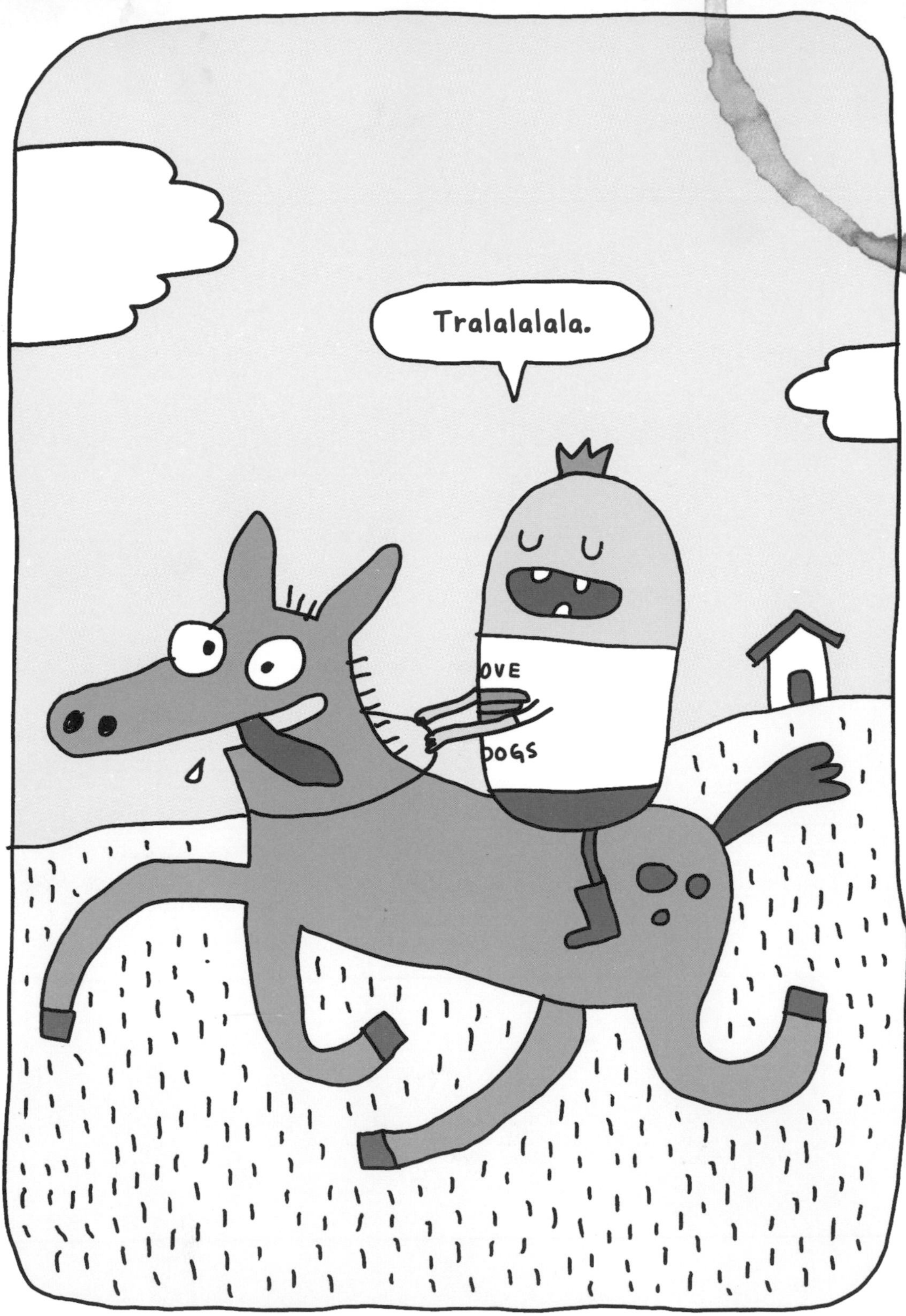
Tralalalala.
OVE
DOGS

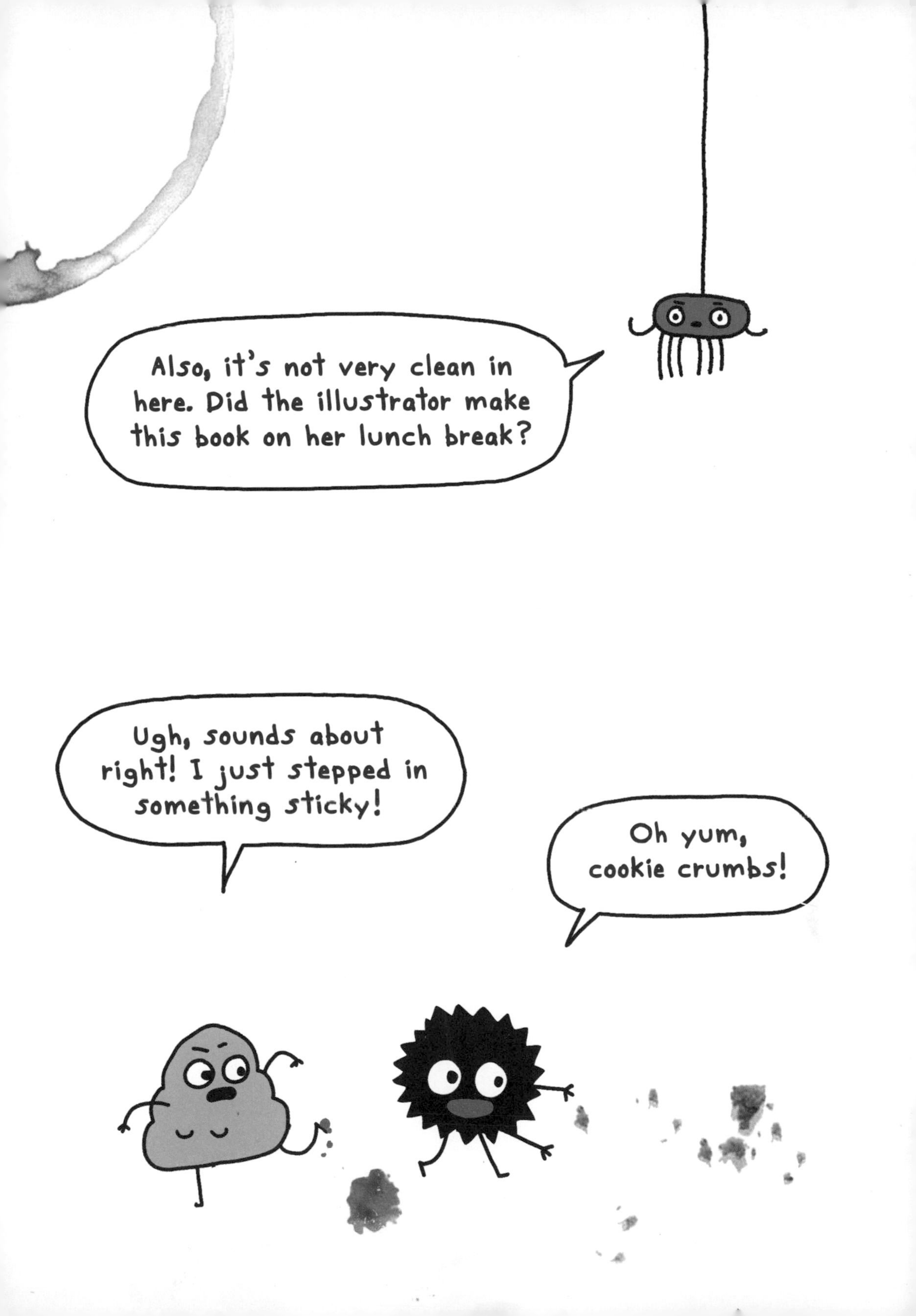
Also, it's not very clean in here. Did the illustrator make this book on her lunch break?
Ugh, sounds about right! I just stepped in something sticky!
Oh yum, cookie crumbs!

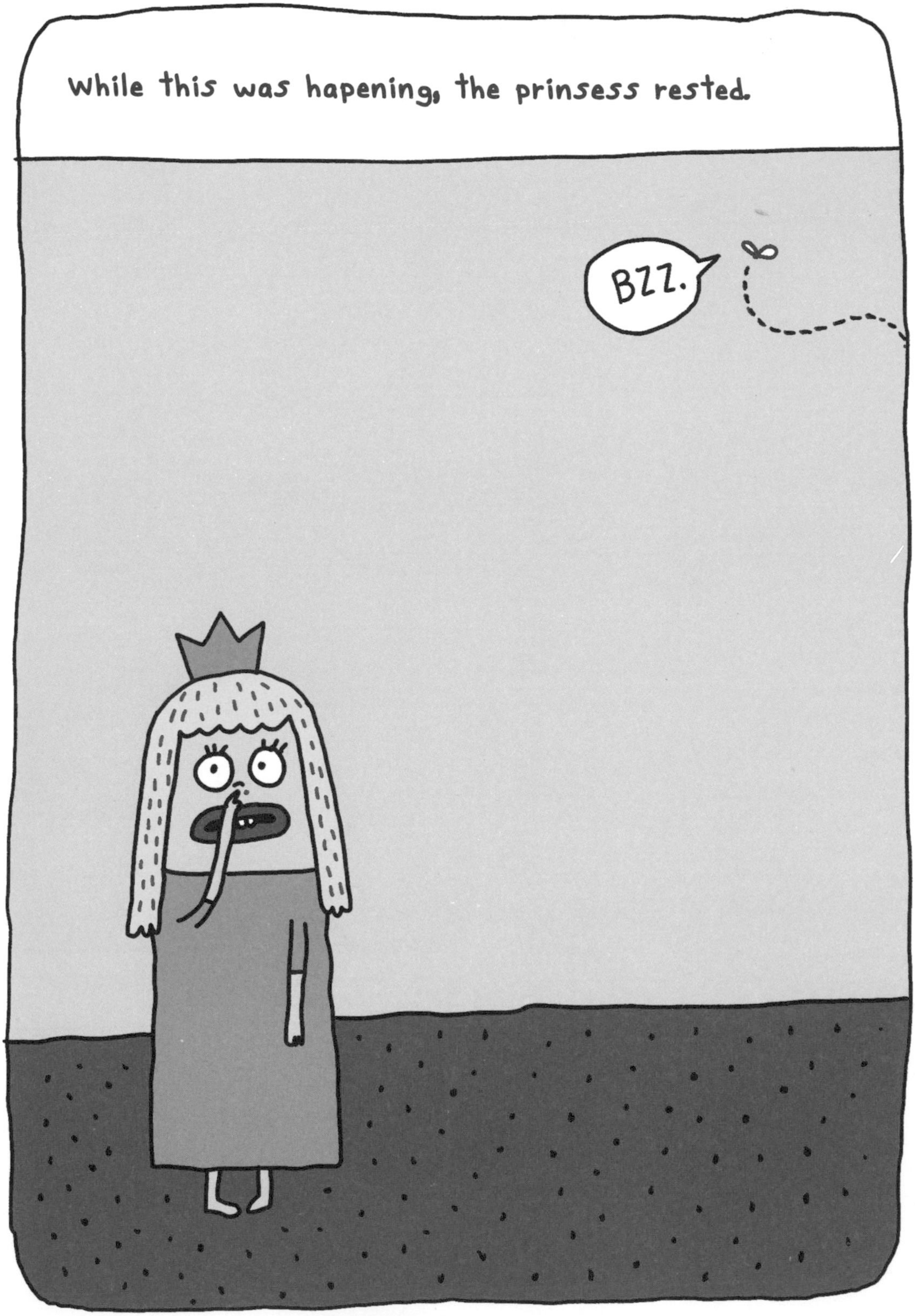
While this was hapening, the prinsess rested.
BZZ.

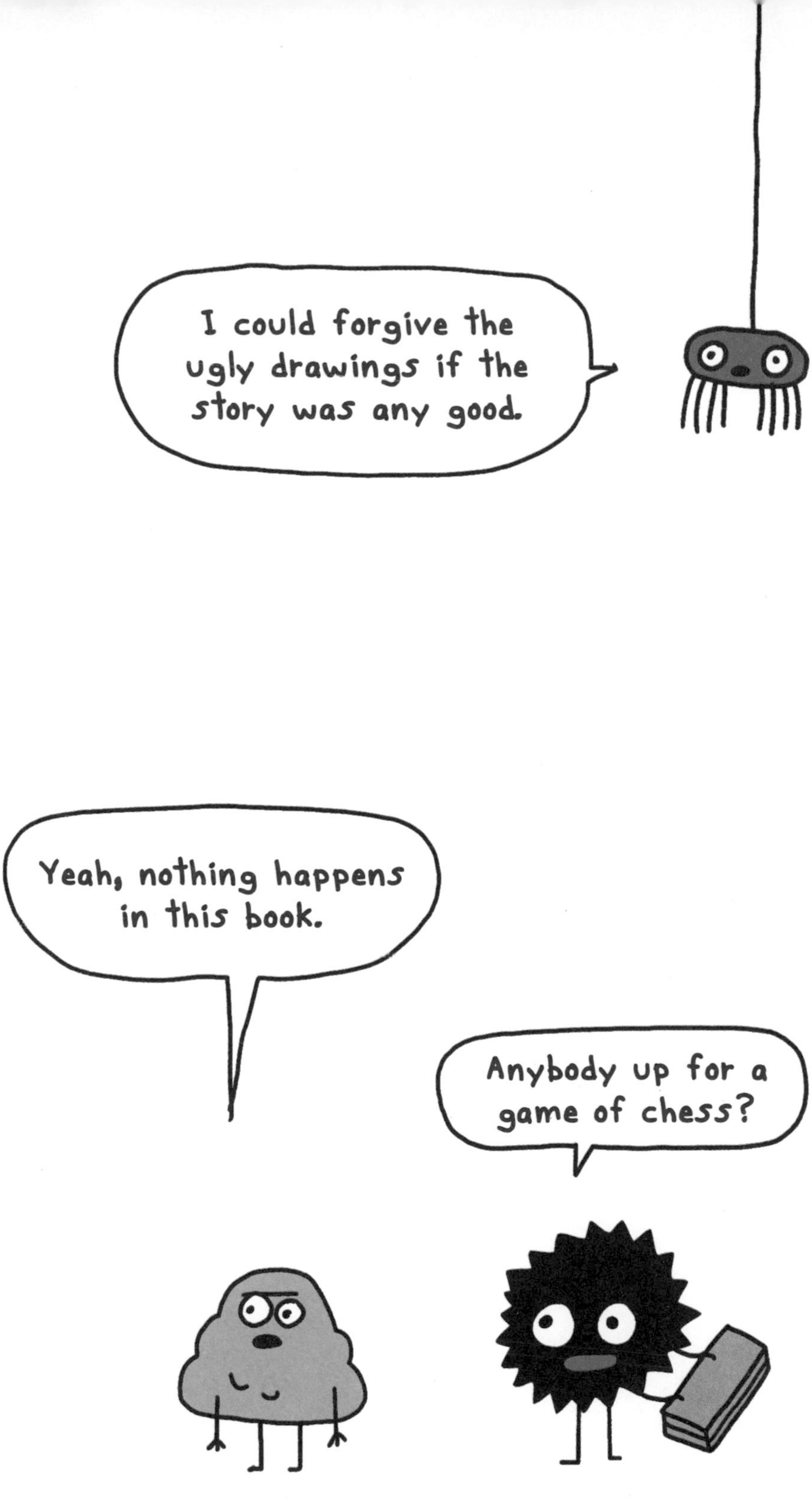
I could forgive the ugly drawings if the story was any good.
Yeah, nothing happens in this book.
Anybody up for a game of chess?

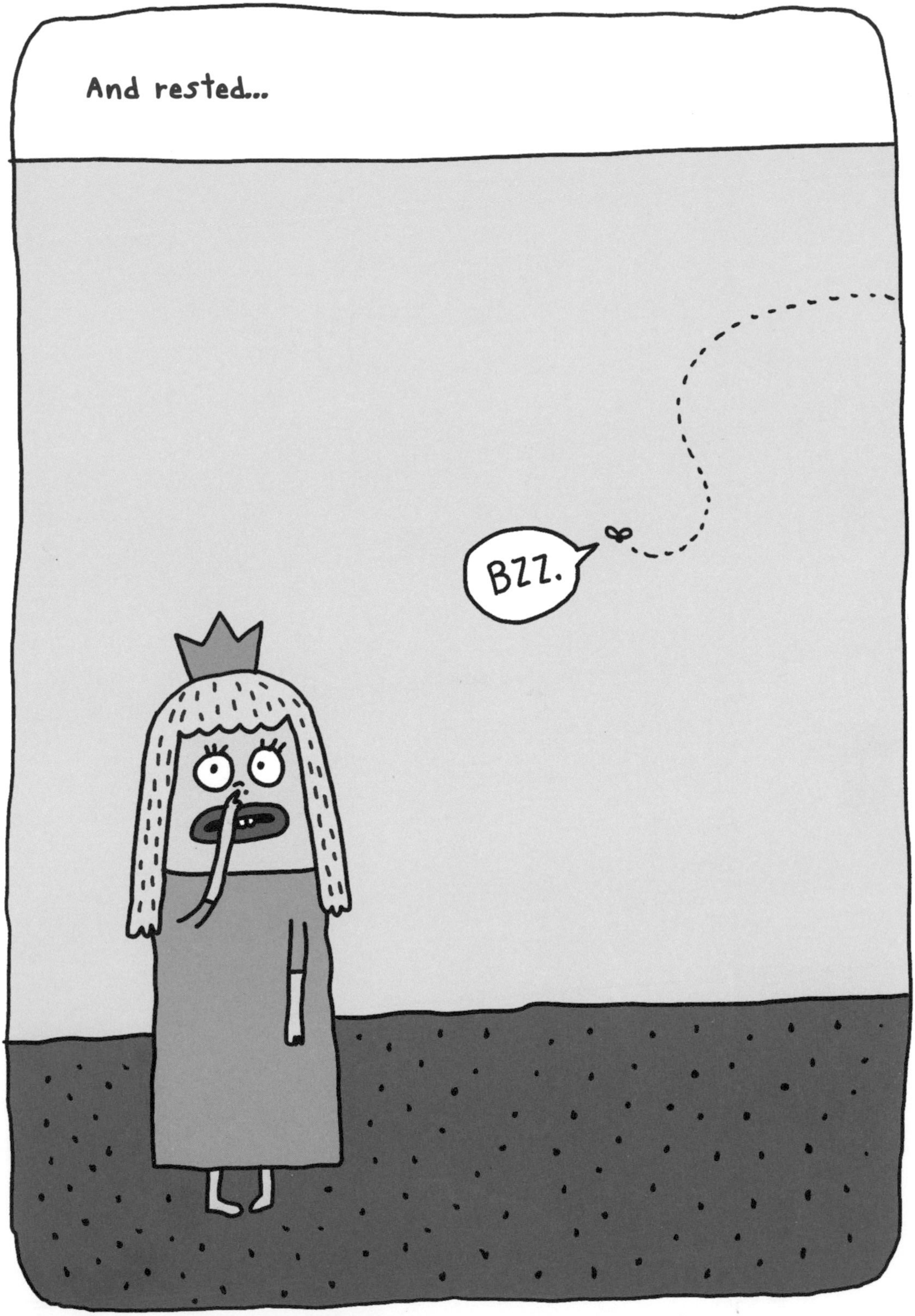
And rested...
BZZ.

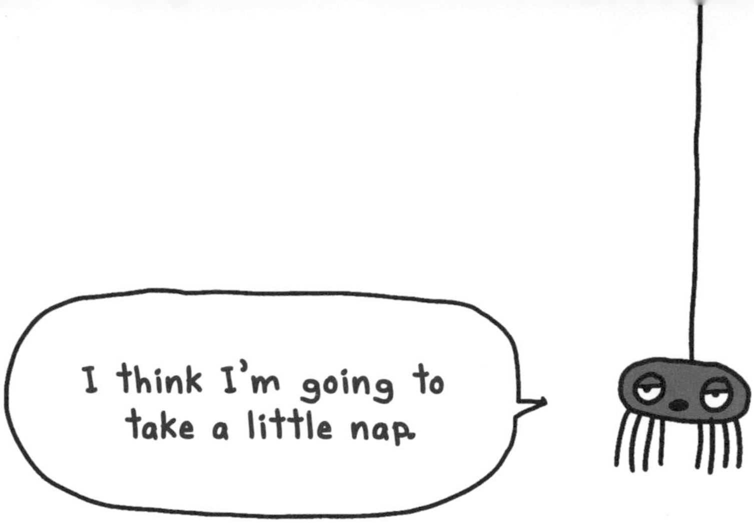
I think I'm going to take a little nap.

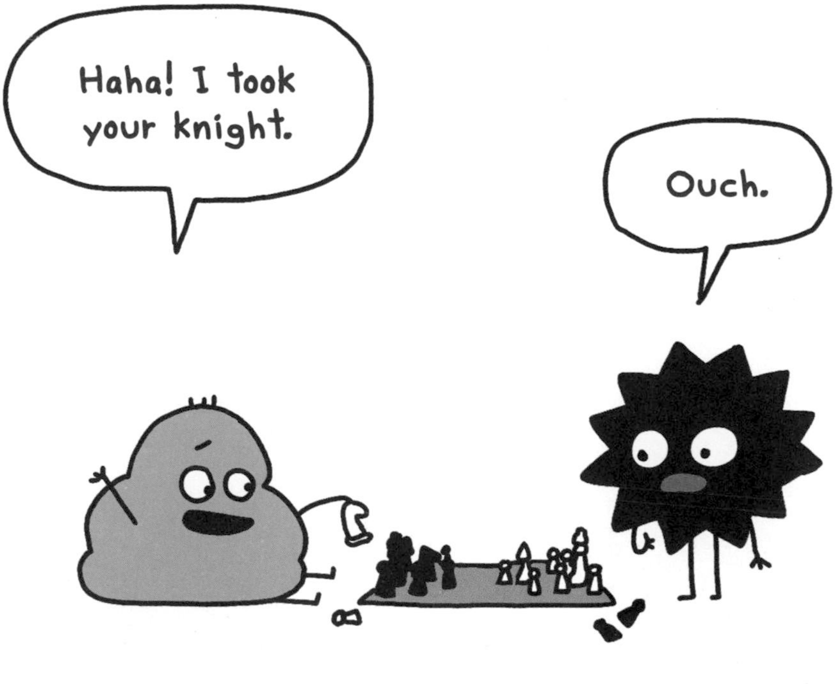
Haha! I took your knight.
Ouch.

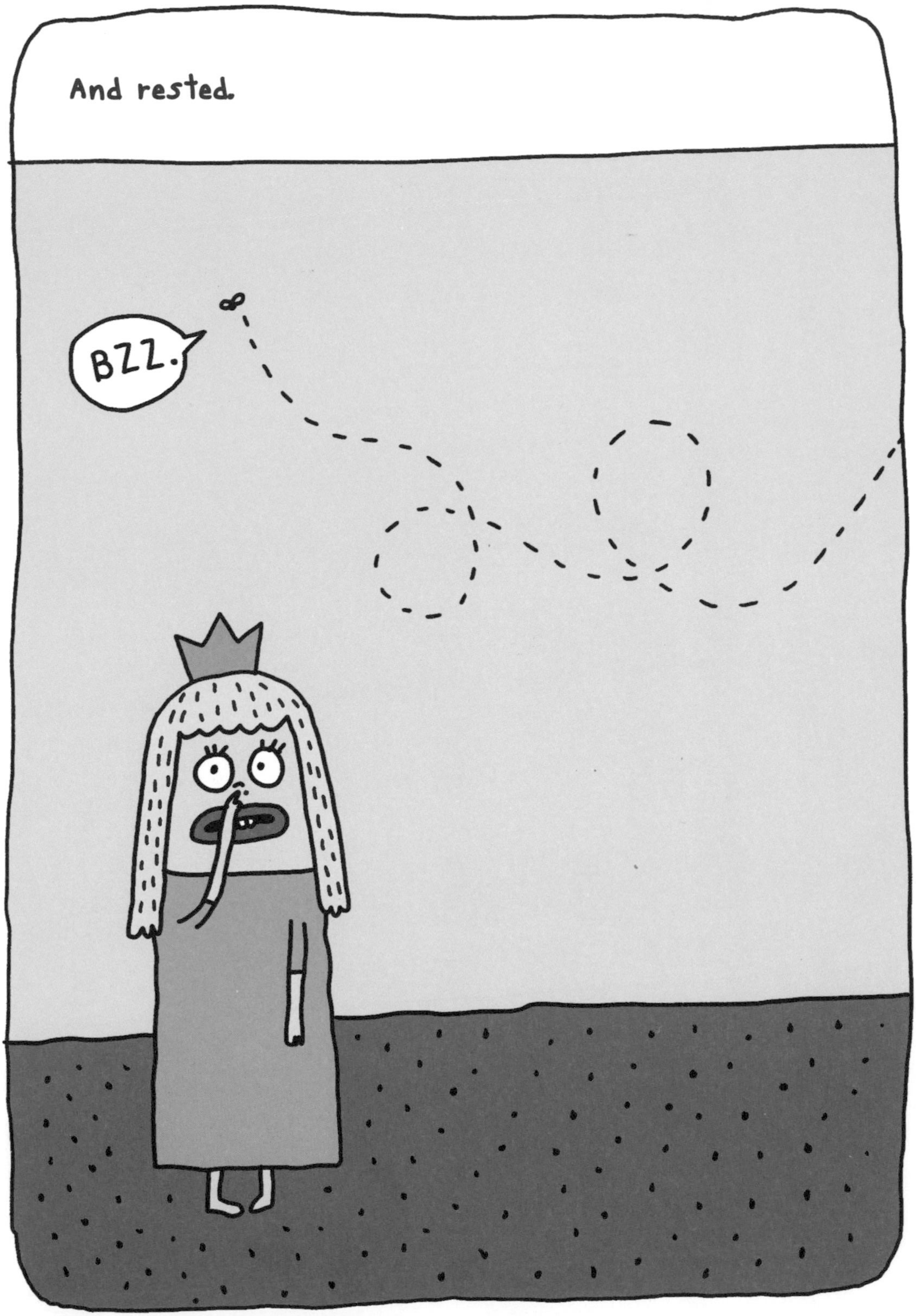
And rested.
BZZ.

Yawnnn. Should we check back in on the story?

Aww, but this is so much more fun!
Haha, it is! Checkmate.

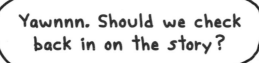

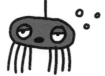

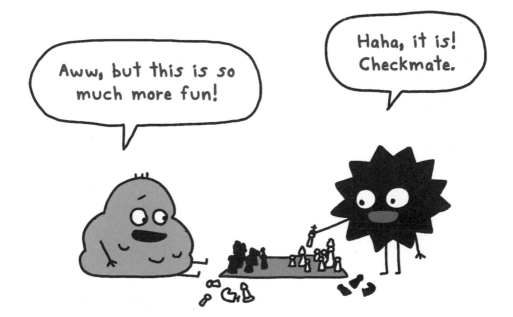

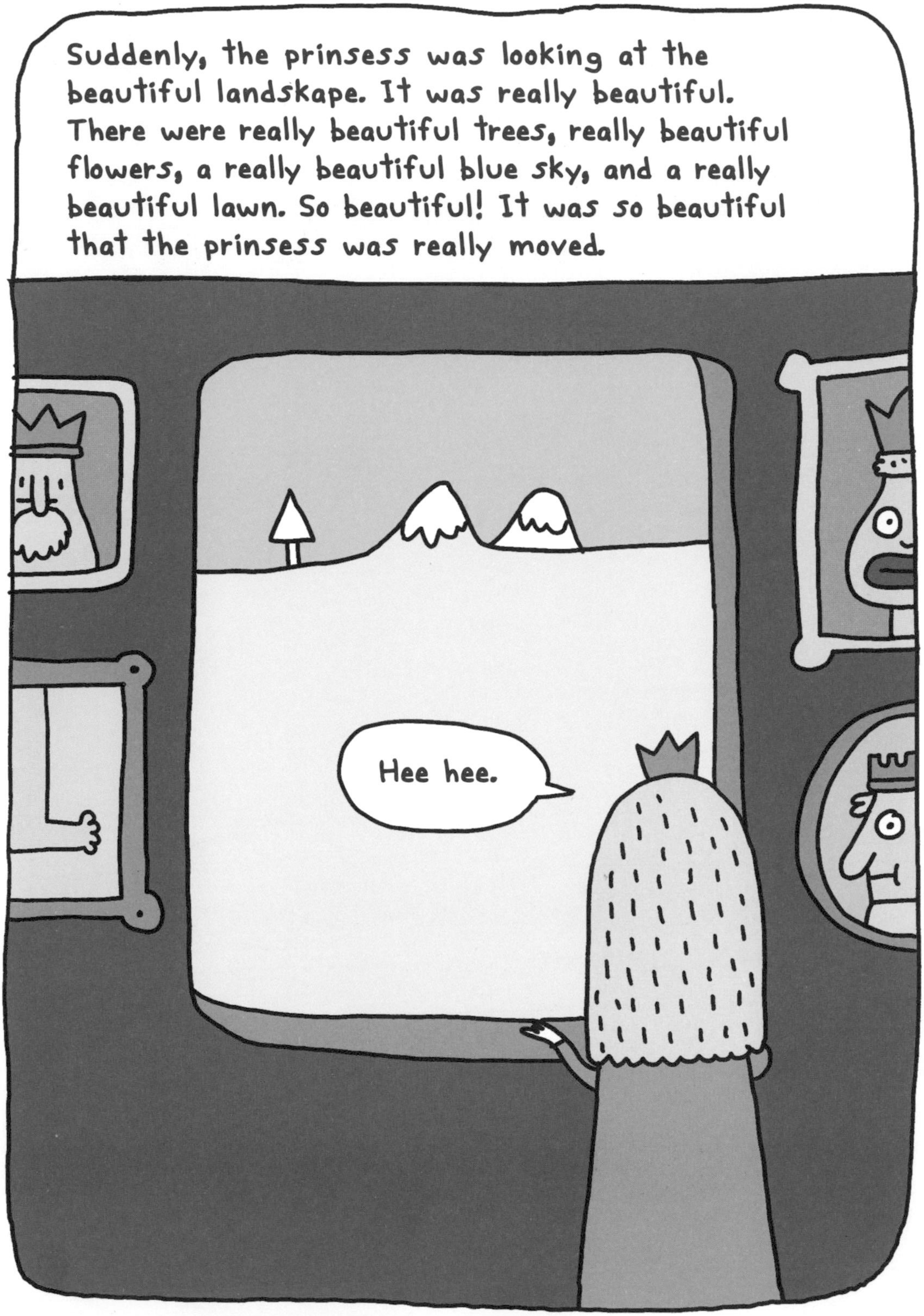
Suddenly, the prinsess was looking at the beautiful landskape. It was really beautiful. There were really beautiful trees, really beautiful flowers, a really beautiful blue sky, and a really beautiful lawn. So beautiful! It was so beautiful that the prinsess was really moved.
Hee hee.

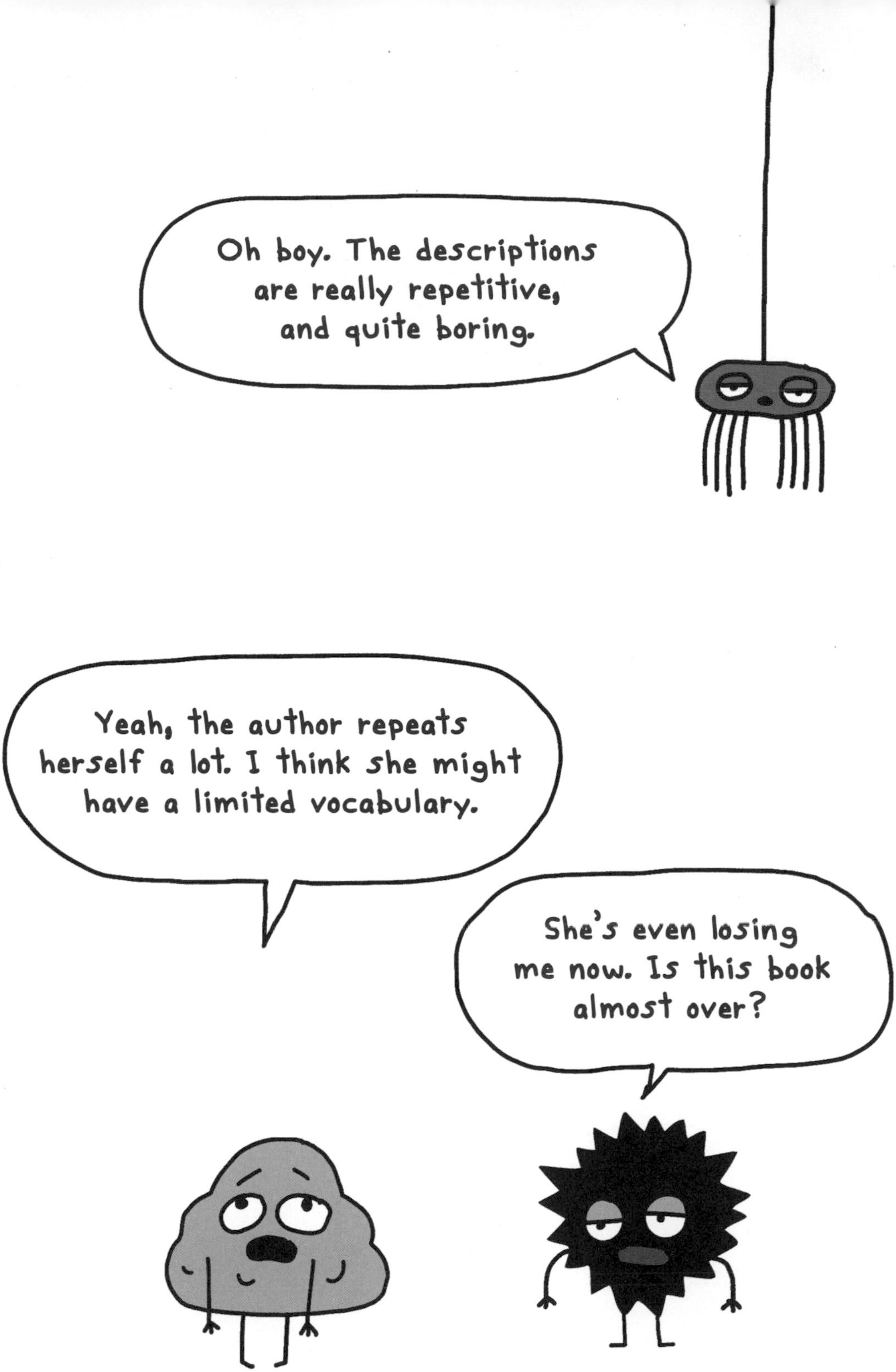
Oh boy. The descriptions are really repetitive, and quite boring.
Yeah, the author repeats herself a lot. I think she might have a limited vocabulary.
She's even losing me now. Is this book almost over?

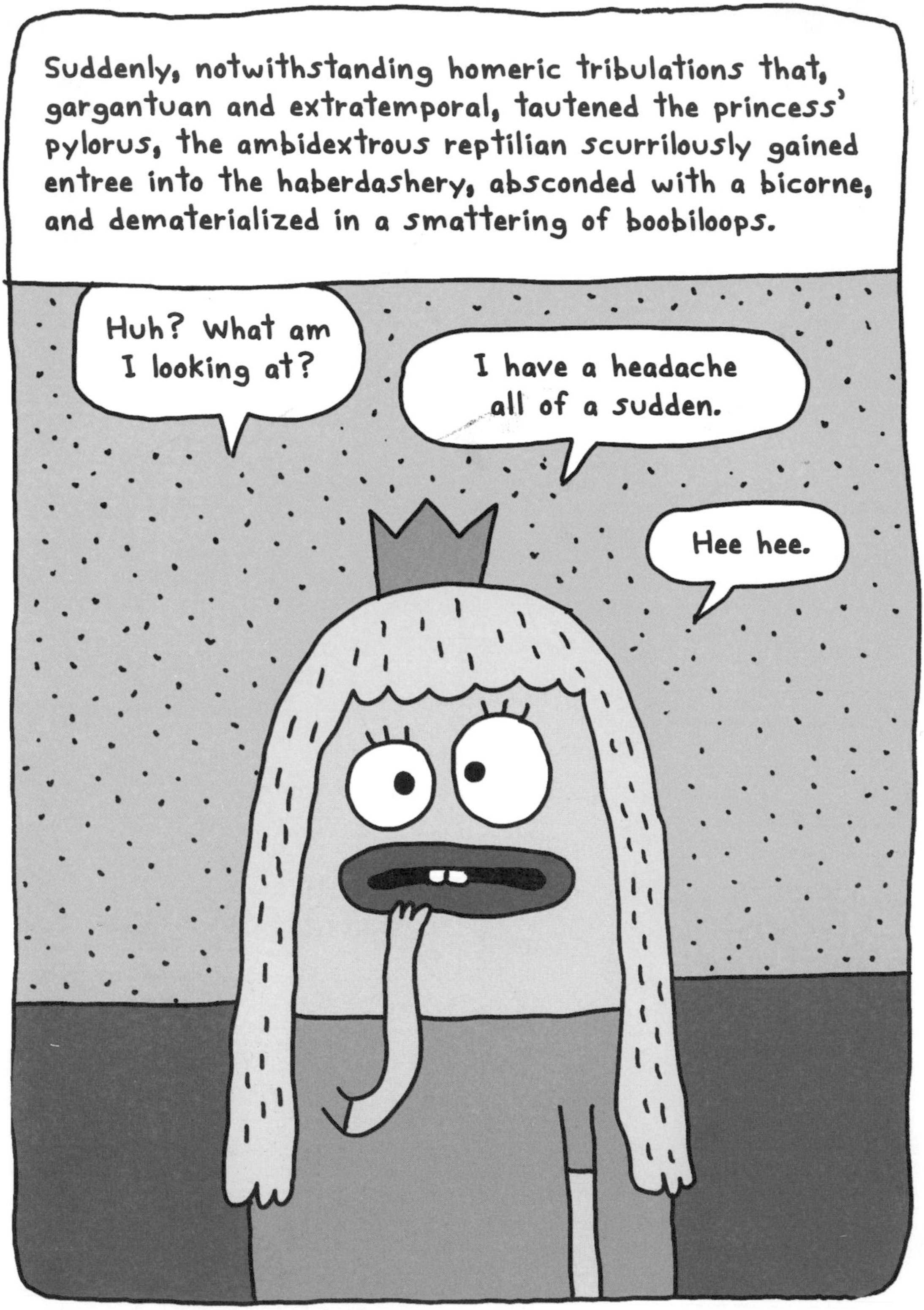
Suddenly, notwithstanding homeric tribulations that, gargantuan and extratemporal, tautened the princess' pylorus, the ambidextrous reptilian scurrilously gained entree into the haberdashery, absconded with a bicorne, and dematerialized in a smattering of boobiloops.
Huh? What am I looking at?
I have a headache all of a sudden.
Hee hee.

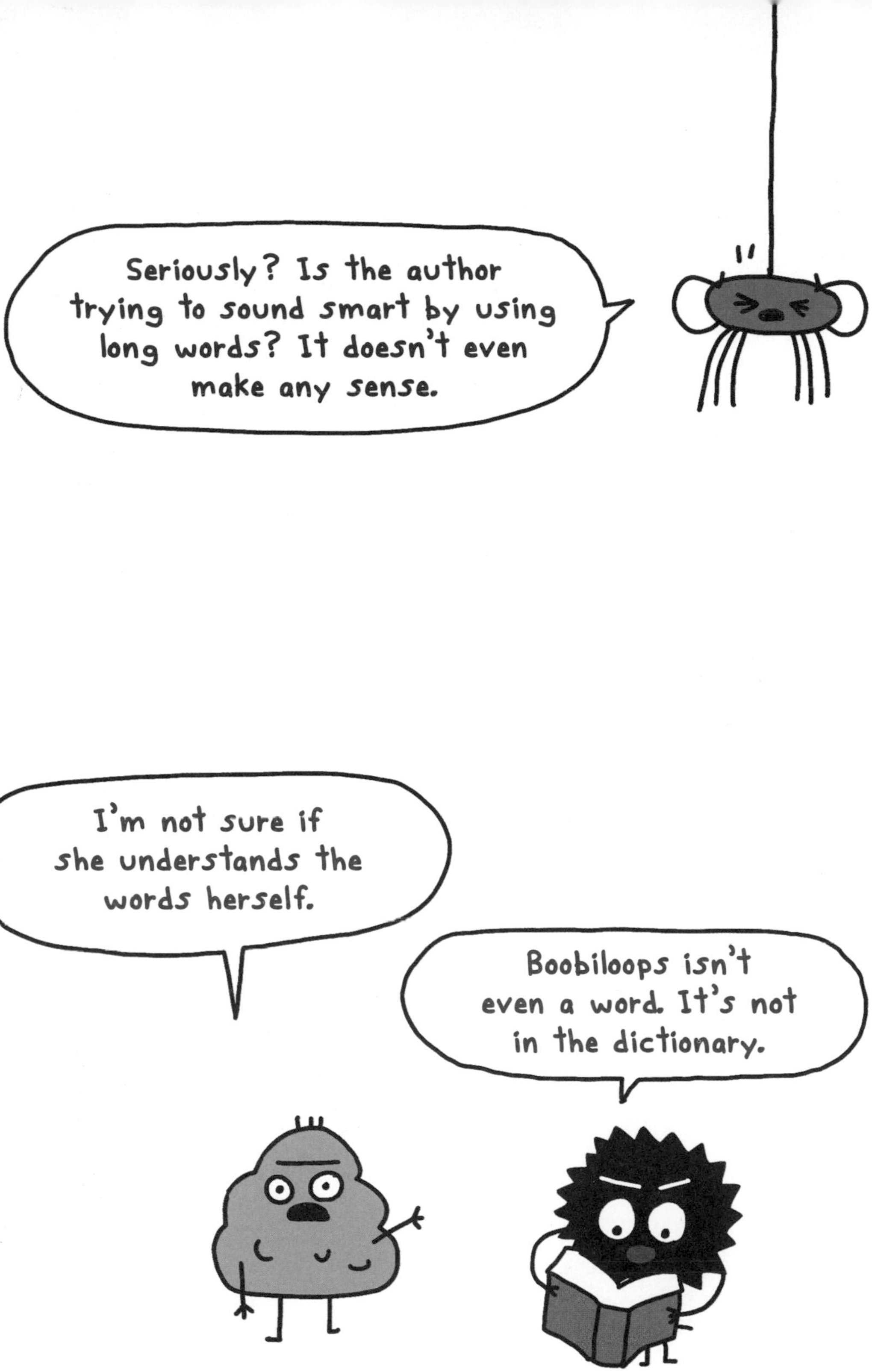
Seriously? Is the author trying to sound smart by using long words? It doesn't even make any sense.
I'm not sure if she understands the words herself.
Boobiloops isn't even a word. It's not in the dictionary.

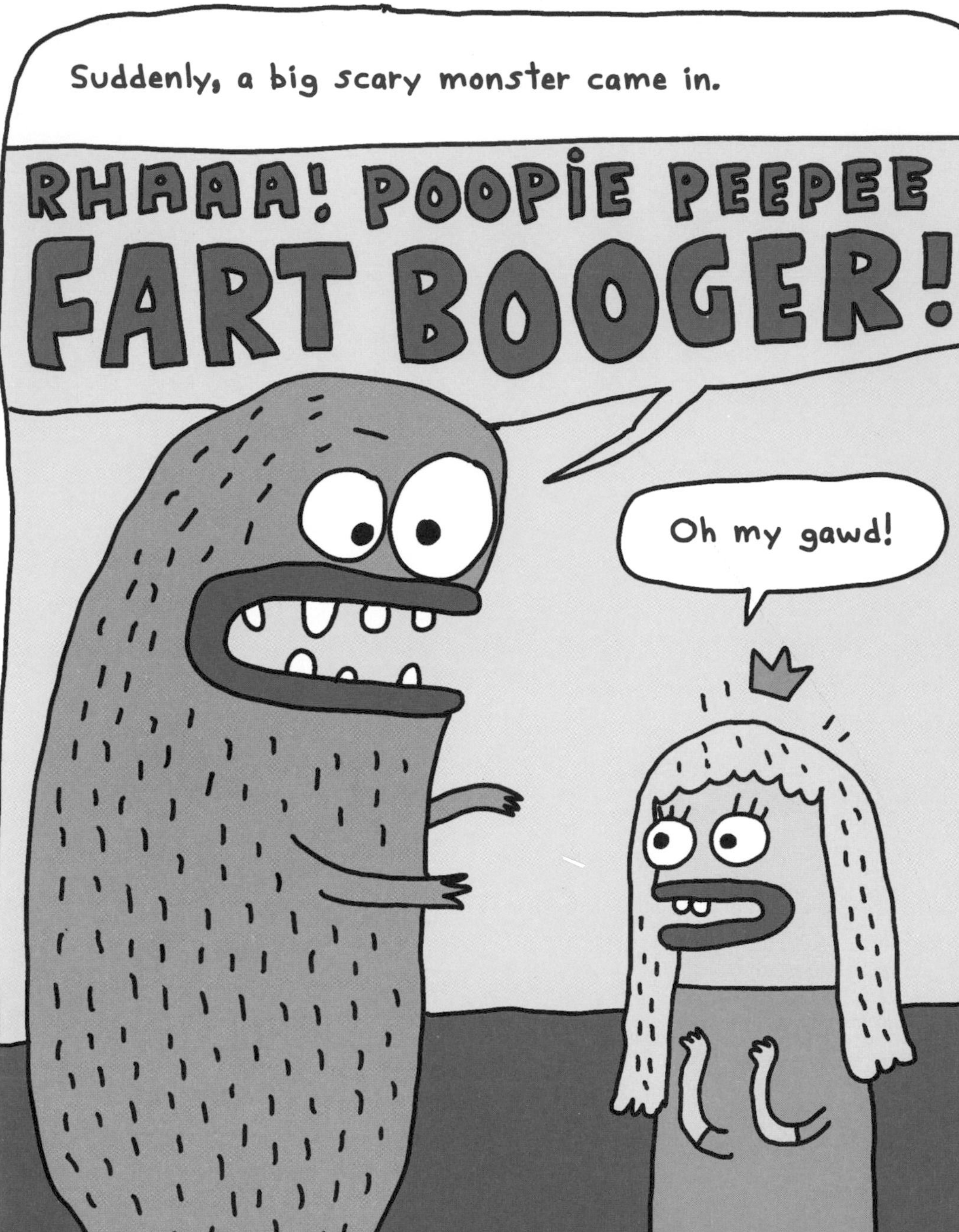
Suddenly, a big scary monster came in.
RHAAA! POOPIE PEEPEE FART BOOGER!
Oh my gawd!

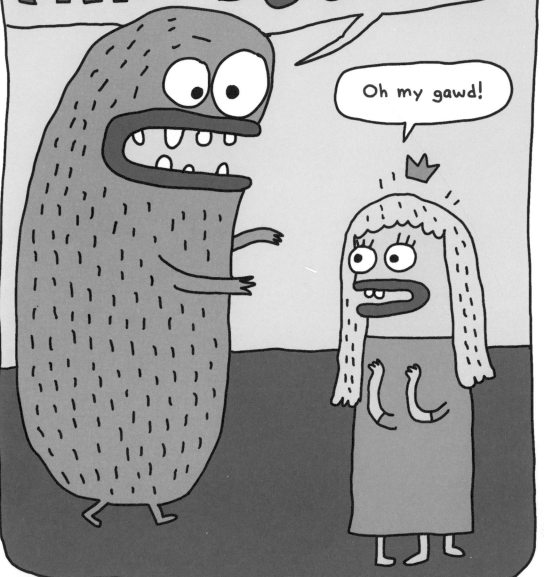

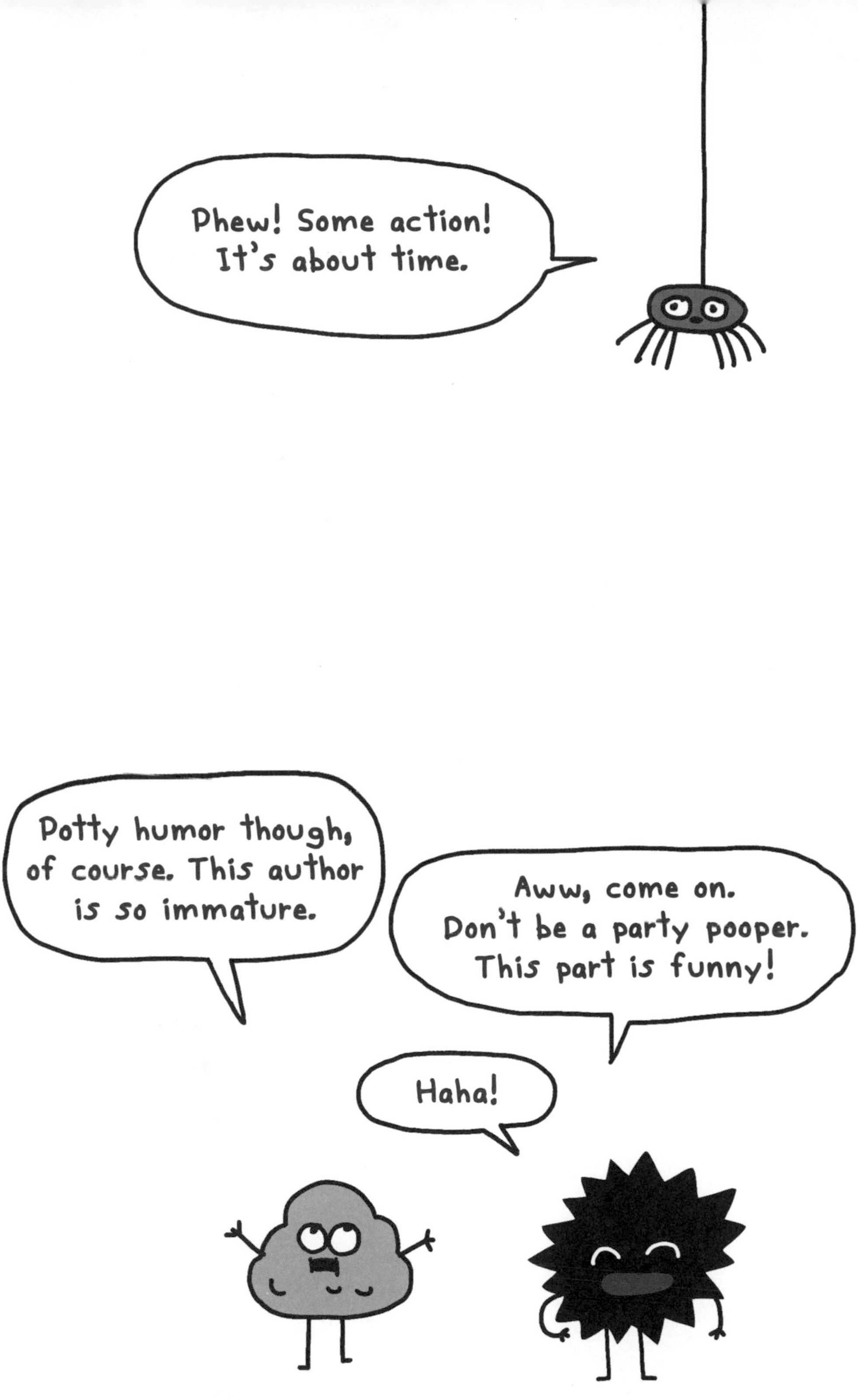
Phew! Some action! It's about time.
Potty humor though, of course. This author is so immature.
Aww, come on. Don't be a party pooper. This part is funny!
Haha!

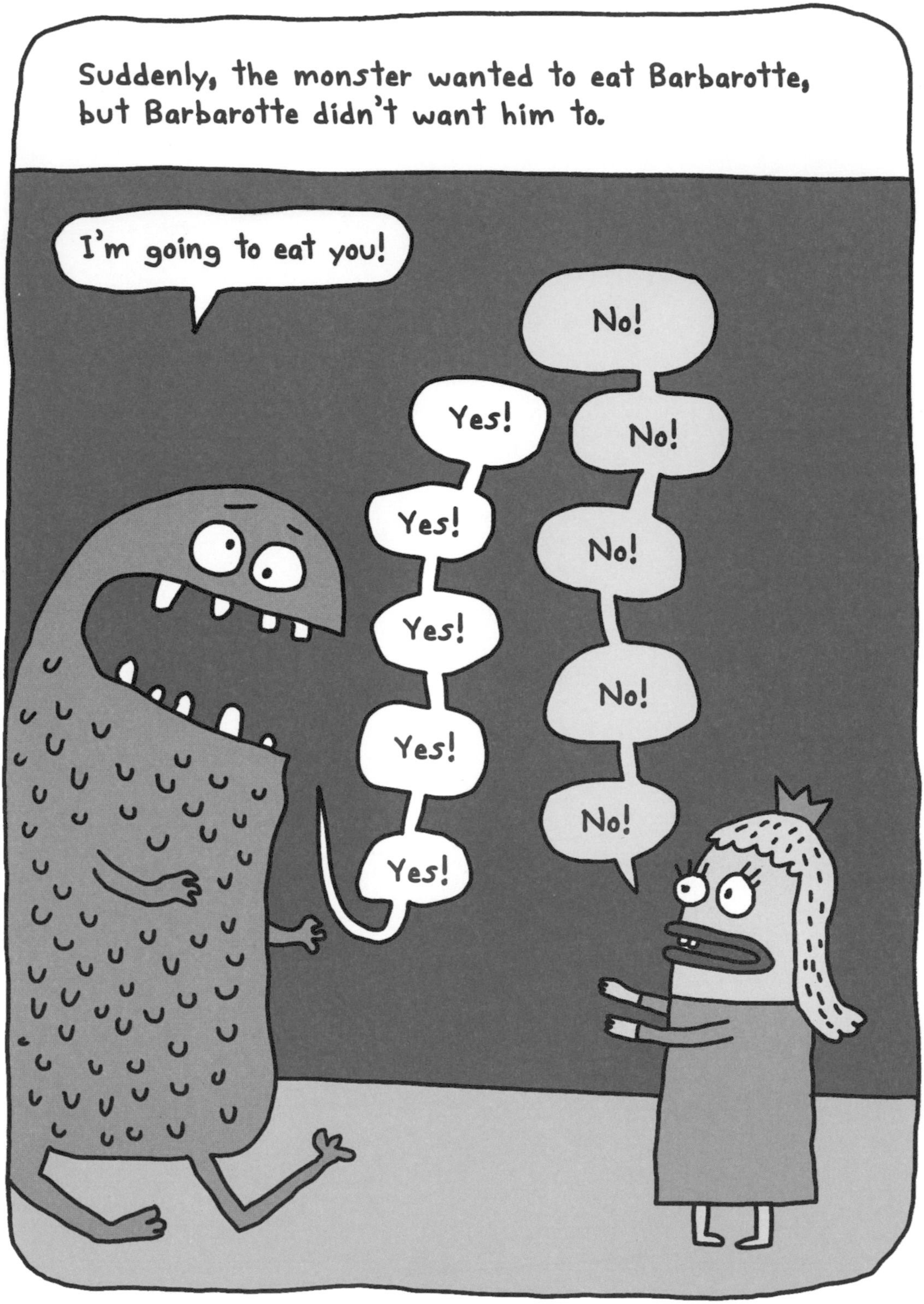

Suddenly, the monster wanted to eat Barbarotte, but Barbarotte didn't want him to.
I'm going to eat you!
Yes!
Yes!
Yes!
Yes!
Yes!
No!
No!
No!
No!
No!

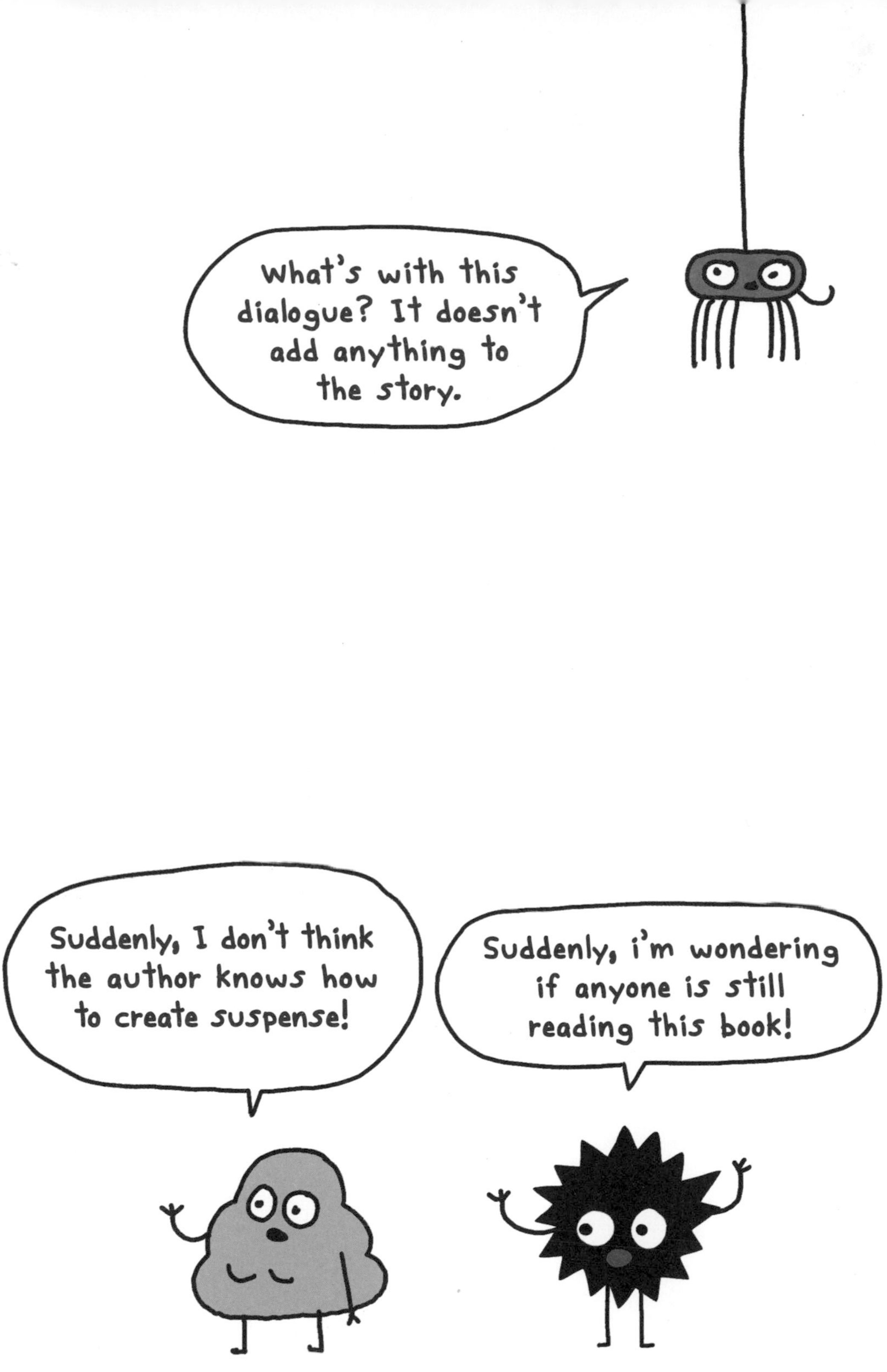
What's with this dialogue? It doesn't add anything to the story.
Suddenly, I don't think the author knows how to create suspense!
Suddenly, i'm wondering if anyone is still reading this book!

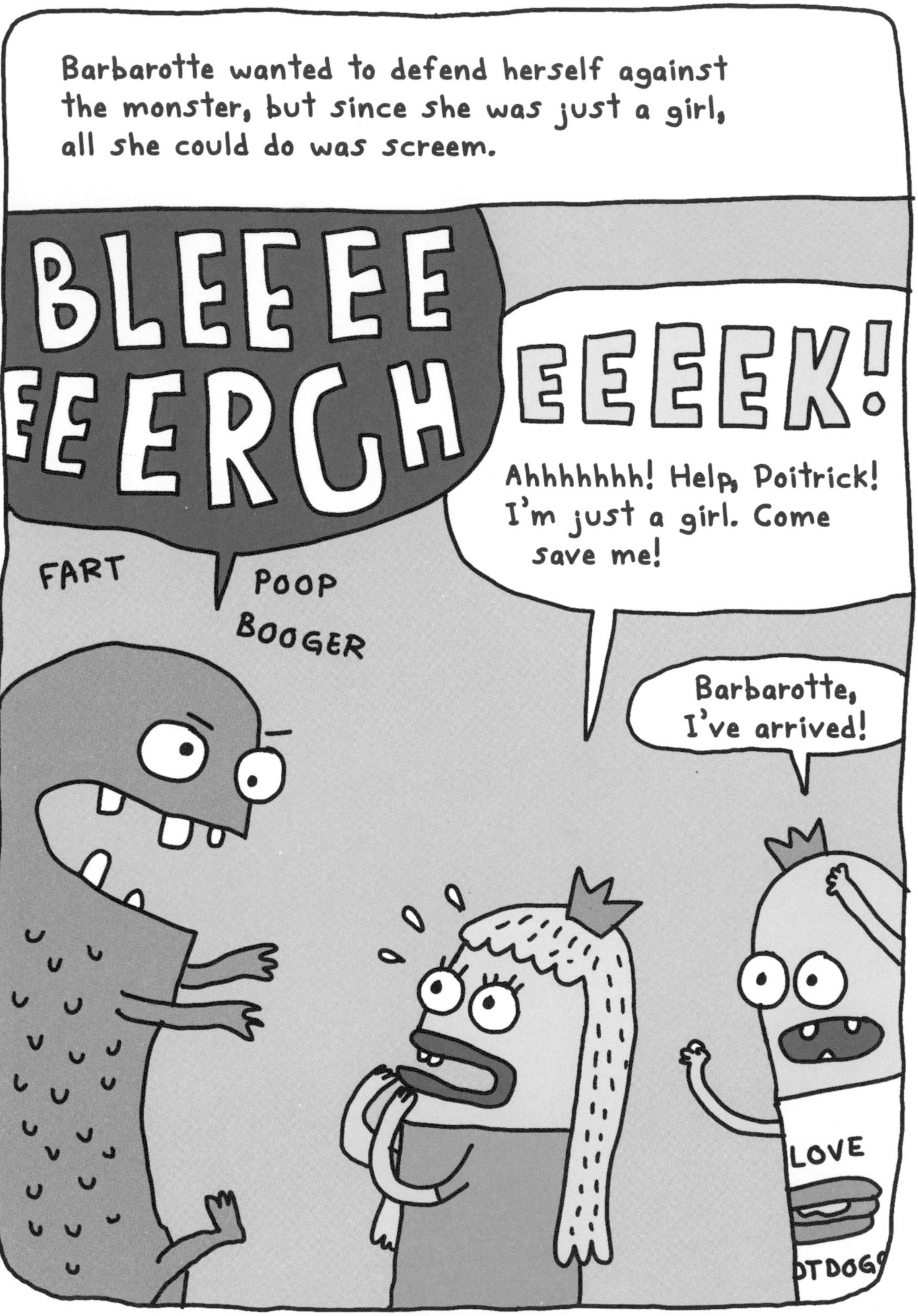
Barbarotte wanted to defend herself against the monster, but since she was just a girl, all she could do was screem.
BLEEEE
EEERGH
FART
POOP
BOOGER
EEEEK!
Ahhhhhhh! Help, Poitrick! I'm just a girl. Come save me!
Barbarotte, I've arrived!
LOVE

Oh no. On top of everything else, this book is sexist too?

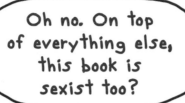

Barbarotte barely had any dialogue the whole story— the author finally gives her some and it's this?

Come on, Barbarotte! It's not 1850! You don't need a man to save you!

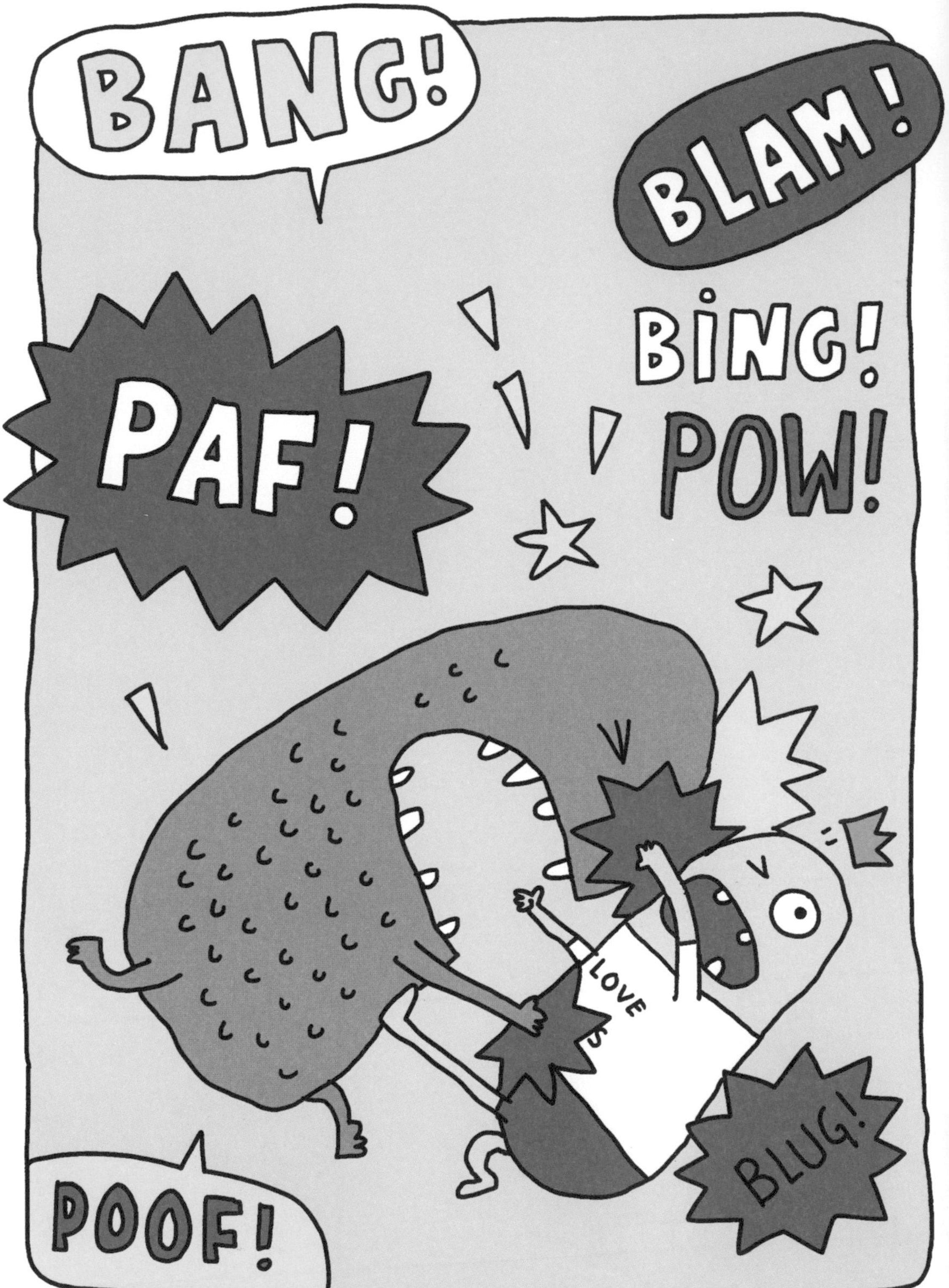
BANG!
BLAM!
PAF!
BING!
POW!
LOVE
POOF!
BLUG!

Okay, gratuitous violence. Very original.

Now, now boys. Use your words.
Oh dear, I hope they don't hurt themselves.

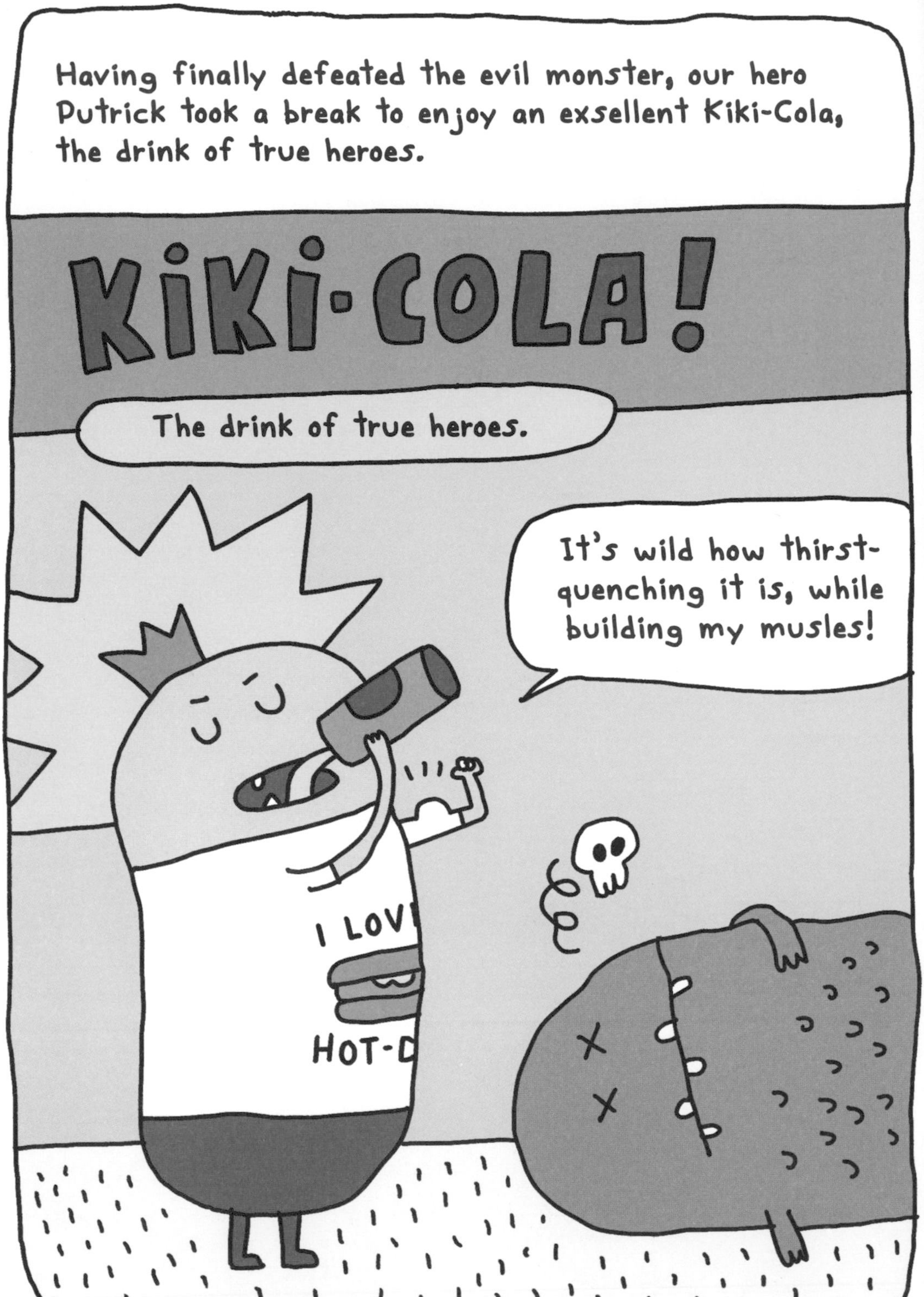
Having finally defeated the evil monster, our hero Putrick took a break to enjoy an exsellent Kiki-Cola, the drink of true heroes.
KiKi-COLA!
The drink of true heroes.
It's wild how thirst-quenching it is, while building my musles!
I LOV
HOT-D

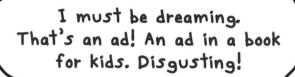

I must be dreaming. That's an ad! An ad in a book for kids. Disgusting!

Isn't that illegal?

♫

PSHiiT!

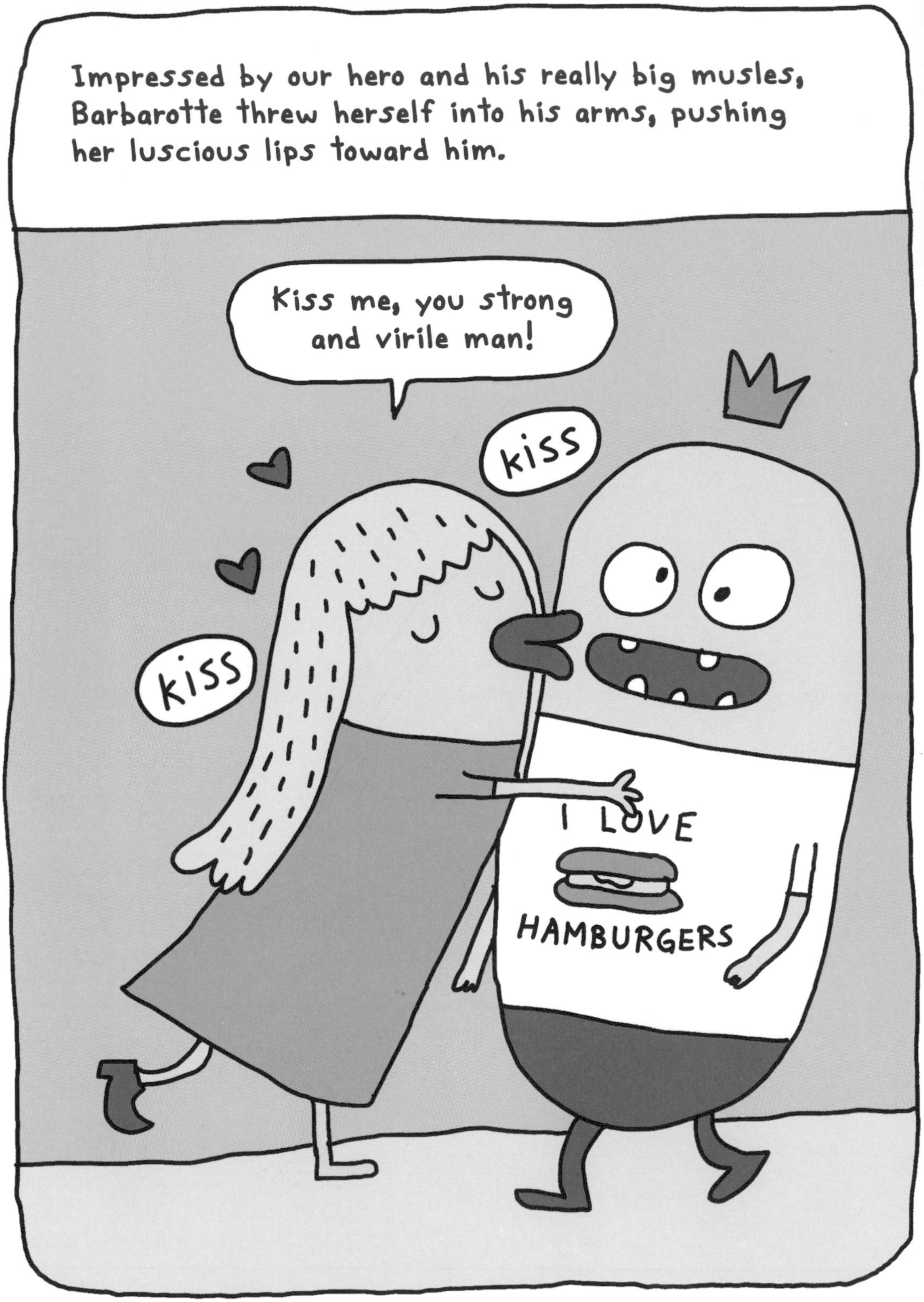
Impressed by our hero and his really big musles, Barbarotte threw herself into his arms, pushing her luscious lips toward him.
Kiss me, you strong and virile man!
kiss
kiss
I LOVE HAMBURGERS

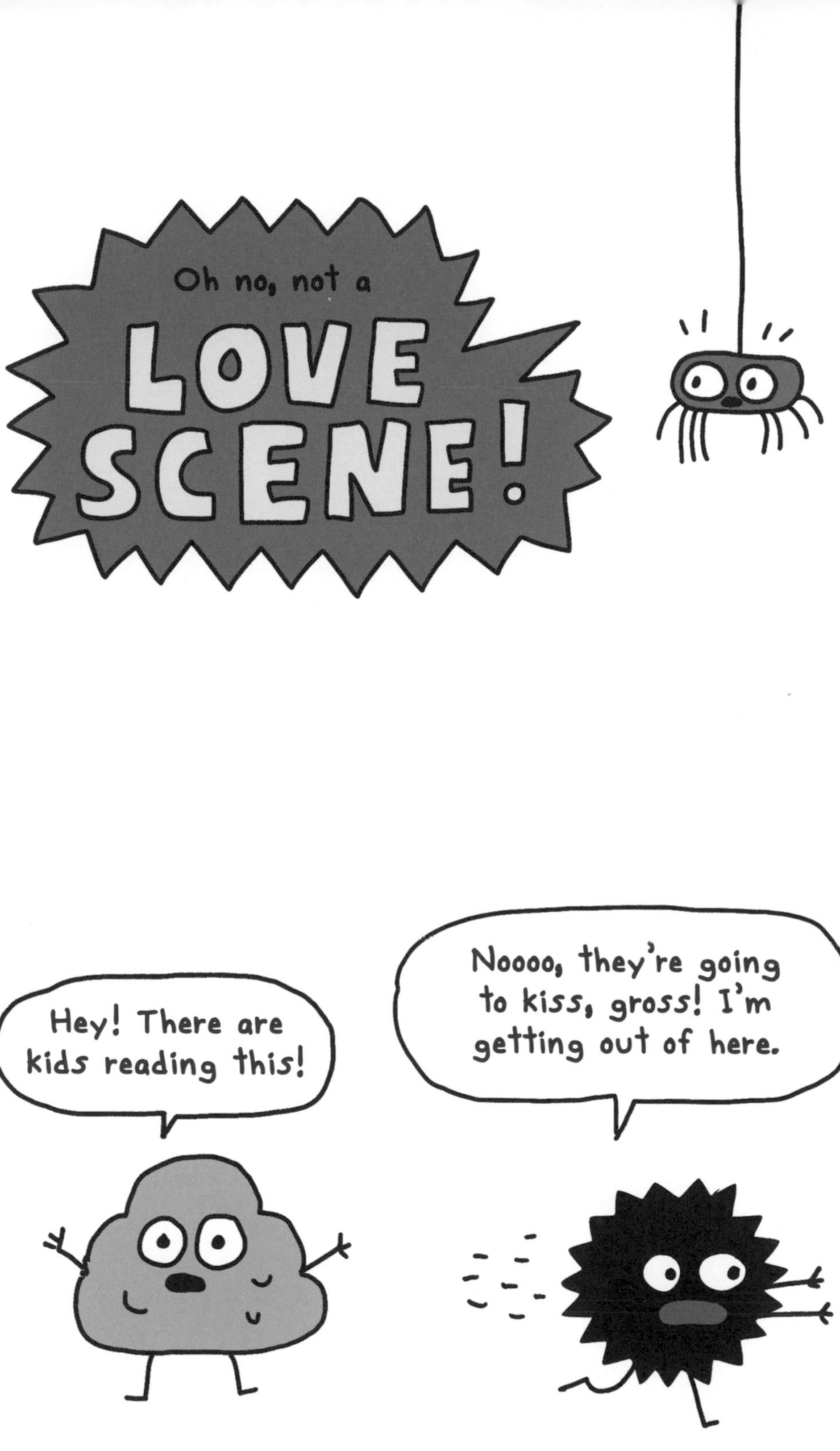
Oh no, not a
LOVE SCENE!
Hey! There are kids reading this!
Noooo, they're going to kiss, gross! I'm getting out of here.

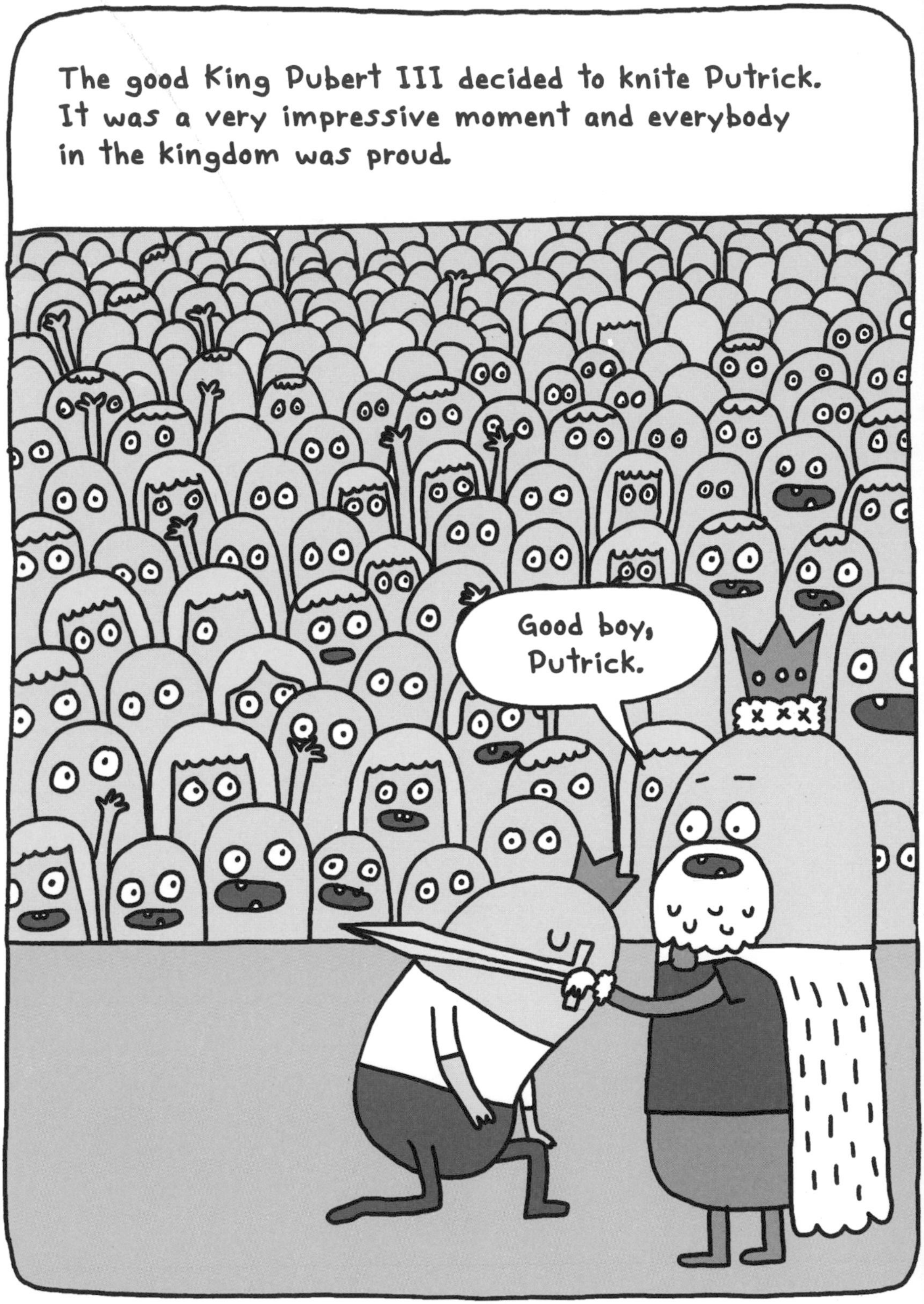
The good King Pubert III decided to knite Putrick. It was a very impressive moment and everybody in the kingdom was proud.
Good boy, Putrick.

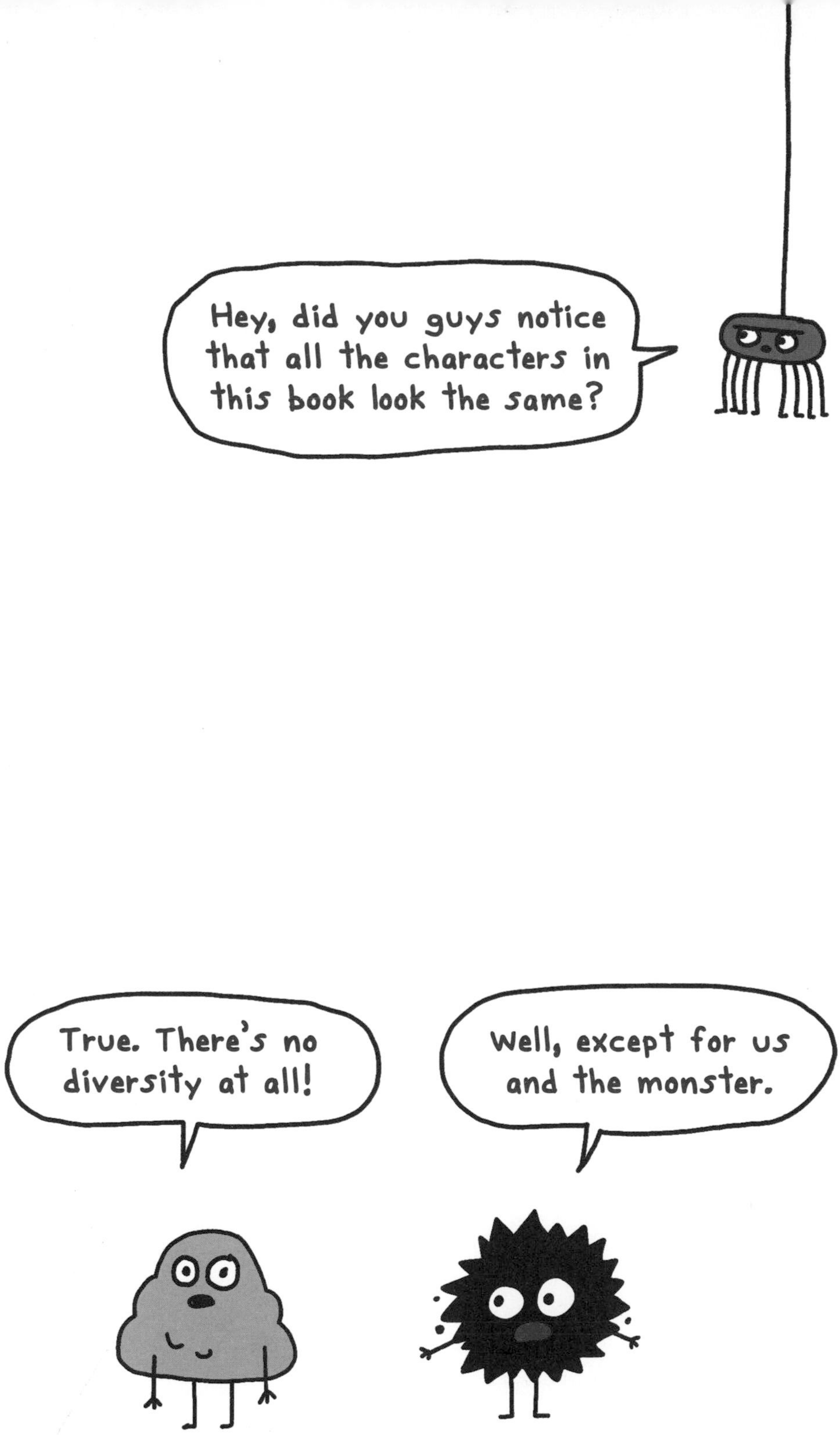
Hey, did you guys notice that all the characters in this book look the same?
True. There's no diversity at all!
Well, except for us and the monster.

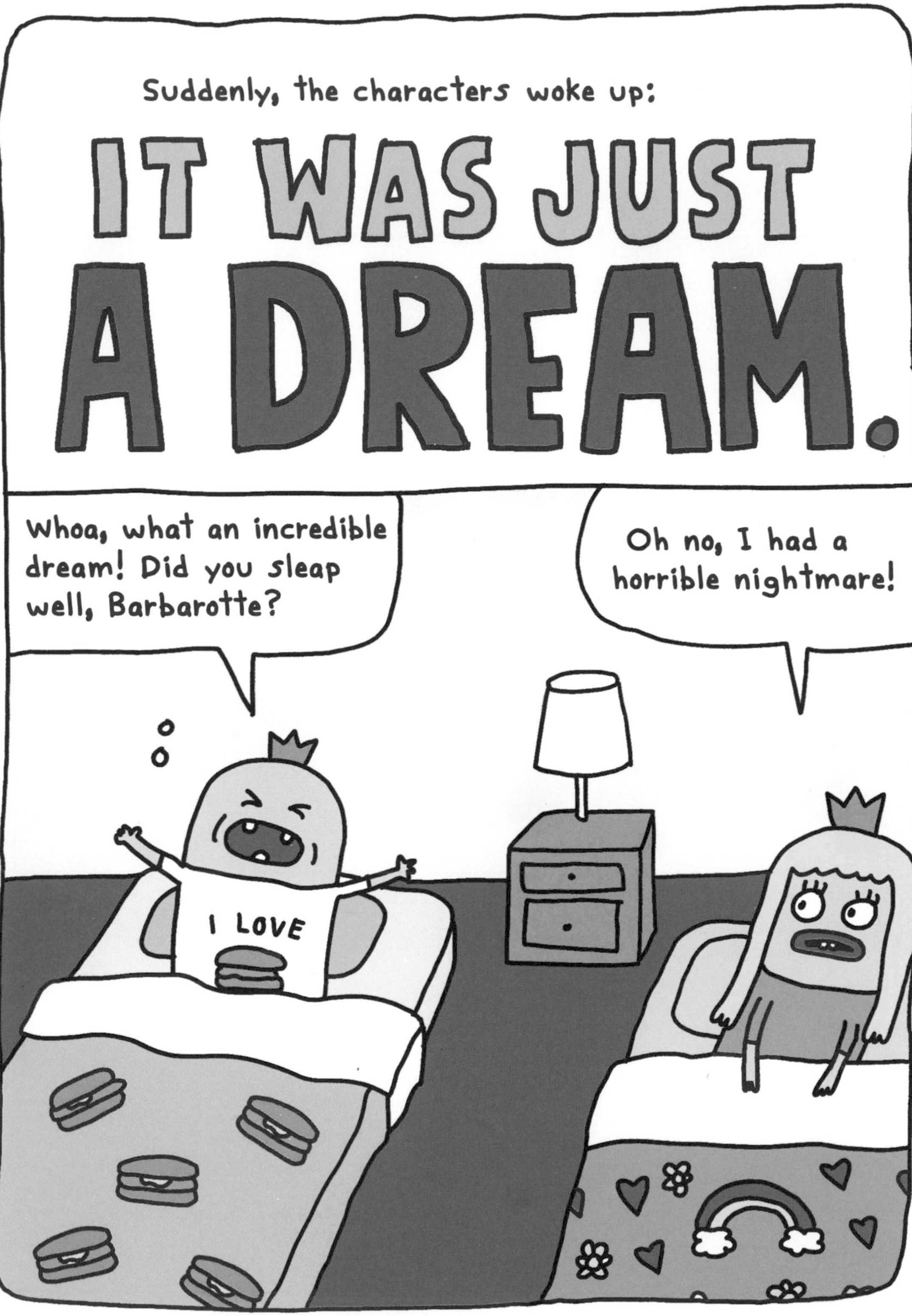
Suddenly, the characters woke up:
IT WAS JUST A DREAM.
Whoa, what an incredible dream! Did you sleap well, Barbarotte?
Oh no, I had a horrible nightmare!
I LOVE

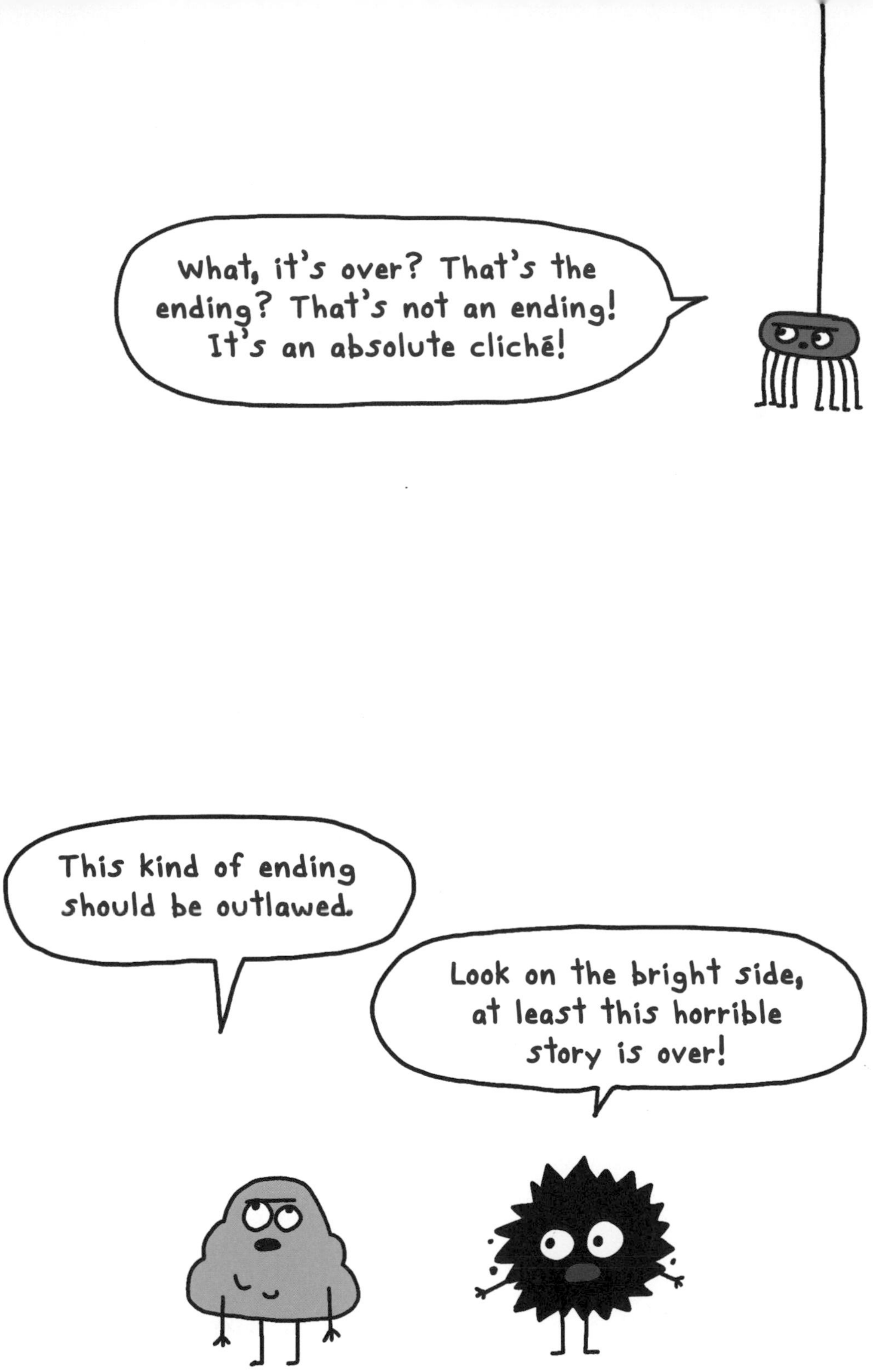
What, it's over? That's the ending? That's not an ending! It's an absolute cliché!
This kind of ending should be outlawed.
Look on the bright side, at least this horrible story is over!

THE
END

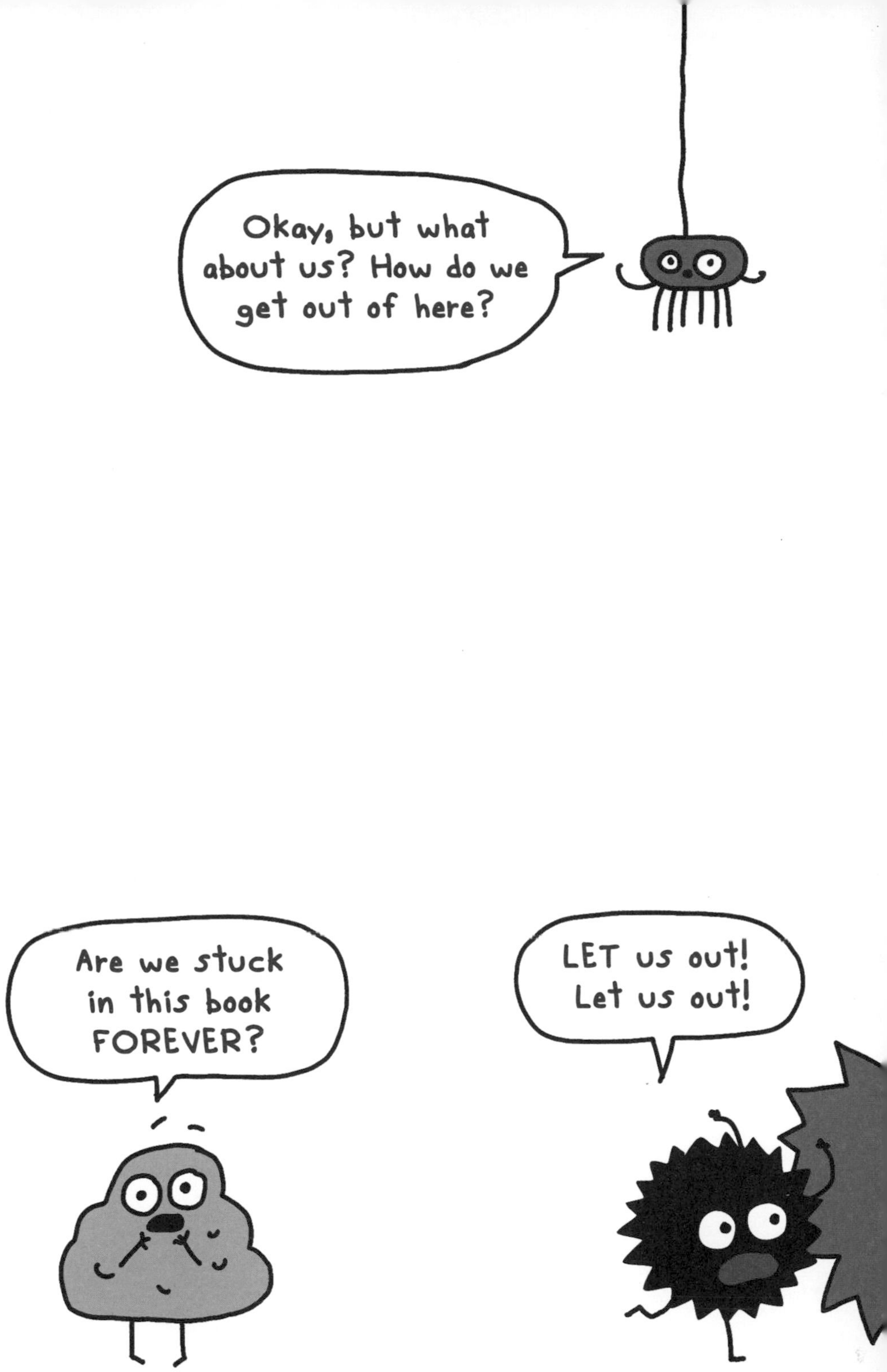
Okay, but what about us? How do we get out of here?
Are we stuck in this book FOREVER?
LET us out! Let us out!

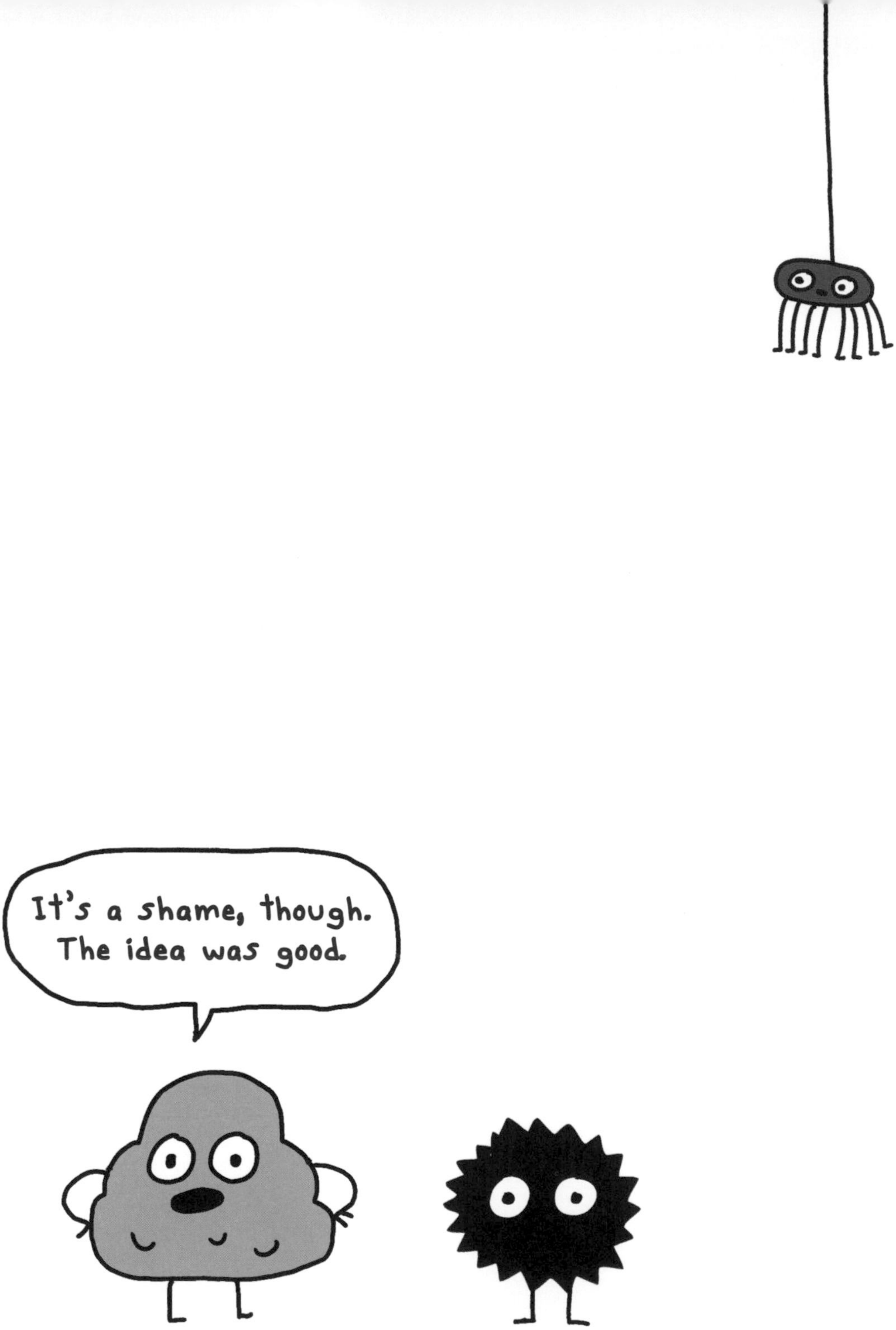
It's a shame, though. The idea was good.

PRINSESS
PRINSE
HAPENING
LANDSKAPE
SCREEM
EXSELLENT
MUSLES
KNITE
SLEAP

Here are the mistakes I found!
Burp!

drawnandquarterly.com | elisegravel.com

978-1-77046-363-9
First edition: May 2019
Printed in China
10 9 8 7 6 5 4 3 2 1

Cataloguing data available from Library and Archives Canada. Hee hee!

Published in the USA by Drawn & Quarterly, a client publisher of Farrar, Straus and Giroux.

Published in Canada by Drawn & Quarterly, client publisher of Raincoast Books.

Published in the United Kingdom by Drawn & Quarterly, a client publisher of Publishers Group UK.

Canadä Drawn & Quarterly acknowledges the support of the Government of Canada and the Canada Council for the Arts for our publishing program.

Drawn & Quarterly reconnaît l'aide financière du gouvernement du Québec par l'entremise de la Société de développement des entreprises culturelles (SODEC) pour nos activités d'édition. Gouvernement du Québec—Programme de crédit d'impôt pour l'édition de livres—Gestion SODEC.

Additional support provided by Kiki-Cola. Get your muscles BIG!

Elise Gravel is an author illustrator from Montreal, Quebec. In 2012, Gravel received the Governor General's Literary Award for her book *La clé à molette*. A prolific artist, she currently has over thirty children's books to her name, which have been translated into a dozen languages, including *The Disgusting Critters* series, *The Mushroom Fan Club*, and *If Found, Please Return to Elise Gravel*, her challenge to young artists to keep a sketchbook. Gravel lives in Montreal with her spouse, two daughters, cats, and a few spiders.

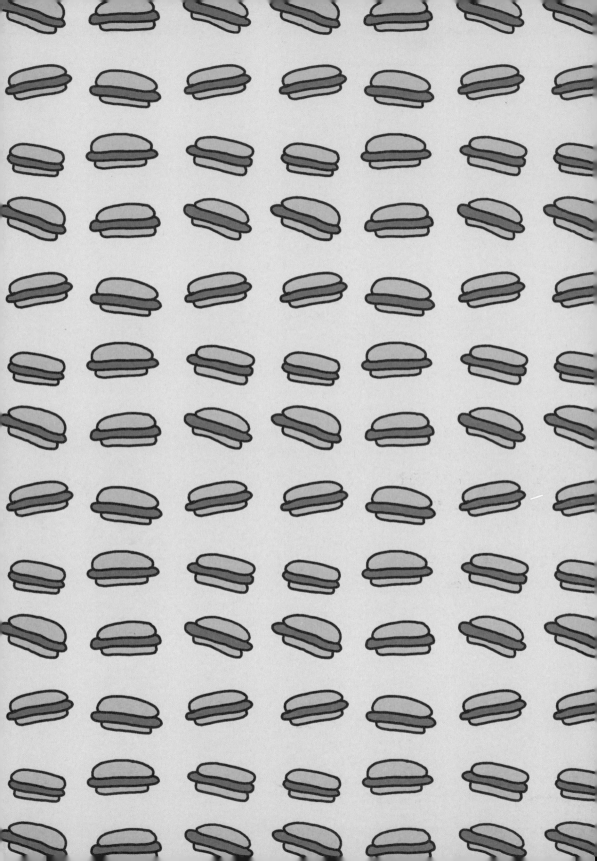